Belle of the Ball

"You need to learn, Miss Portham, I am neither saint nor sinner, I am simply a man."

And I am a woman, she longed to scream, although shyness and fear held her silent. She bit her lip and reached deep down inside herself for the cool self-possession that had served her so well in the past.

"I am aware of that, my lord. And it is to that man I wish to make my apologies. I said terrible things to him and I am hoping he will find it in himself to forgive me. Do you think he will?"

"I am sure he will," he replied, not trusting himself to touch her again. . . .

Other Regency Romances from Avon Books

By Joan Overfield
THE VISCOUNT'S VIXEN

By Nancy Richards-Akers
LADY SARAH'S CHARADE
MISS WICKHAM'S BETROTHAL

By Jo Beverley
EMILY AND THE DARK ANGEL
THE FORTUNE HUNTER
MY LADY NOTORIOUS
THE STANFORTH SECRETS

By Loretta Chase
THE ENGLISH WITCH
ISABELLA
KNAVES' WAGER
THE SANDALWOOD PRINCESS
VISCOUNT VAGABOND

By Kasey Michaels
THE CHAOTIC MISS CRISPINO
THE DUBIOUS MISS DALRYMPLE
THE HAUNTED MISS HAMPSHIRE
THE WAGERED MISS WINSLOW

By Marlene Suson
DEVIL'S BARGAIN
THE FAIR IMPOSTOR

Belle of the Ball

JOAN OVERFIELD

AVON BOOKS ◆ NEW YORK

BELLE OF THE BALL is an original publication of Avon Books. This work has never before appeared in book form. This work is a novel. Any similarity to actual persons or events is purely co-incidental.

AVON BOOKS
A division of   06046457
The Hearst Corporation
1350 Avenue of the Americas
New York, New York 10019

Copyright © 1993 by Joan Overfield
Published by arrangement with the author
Library of Congress Catalog Card Number: 92-97295
ISBN: 0-380-76923-9

First Avon Books Printing: May 1993

AVON TRADEMARK REG. U.S. PAT. OFF. AND IN OTHER COUNTRIES, MARCA REGISTRADA, HECHO EN U.S.A.

Printed in the U.S.A.

RA   10   9   8   7   6   5   4   3   2   1

This book is dedicated to the memory of Jerri Skeen, who fought the good fight with both courage and laughter. Please, if you do nothing else for your loved ones, have a yearly mammogram and examination. You mean more to the world than you may know.

Belle of the Ball

One

London, 1816

"If there is one thing in this life of which one may be reasonably certain," Mrs. Georgiana Larksdale began, turning a steely gaze upon the quiet young woman sitting opposite her, "it is not *if* a disaster may strike, but *when*."

Miss Arabelle Portham glanced up from the tract she'd been perusing, her delicate blond eyebrows gathering in a frown as she puzzled over the dramatic pronouncement. Only seconds before, her distant cousin had been discussing the latest fashions from Bond Street, and now she was uttering prophecies like some latter-day Cassandra. It made no sense, unless . . .

"Ah, I see," she said, her brow clearing as understanding dawned. "Your toe is paining you."

"It is my ankle," Georgiana corrected, lifting the hem of her gown and offering the affected limb for Belle's inspection. "The poor thing has been throbbing like a sore tooth, and I need not tell you what *that* portends."

Indeed she did not, Belle thought, fighting back a smile. For as long as she had known Georgiana (the sister-in-law of one of her numerous cousins), the older woman had held firm to her belief that

1

her body was possessed of preternatural abilities, and a twinge could predict everything from a shower of rain to catastrophes of biblical proportions. She was especially fond of the catastrophes, and Belle knew there was nothing she liked more than when circumstances proved her correct.

"Perhaps it is only the gout," Belle suggested, fixing a pointed glance at the eclair in Georgiana's hand. "Dr. Philiby did warn you to avoid rich foods, did he not?"

"Dr. Philiby is an old fool," Georgiana muttered, although Belle noted she returned the custard-filled pastry to the tray. "I know the gout when I feel it, and this is quite different, I assure you. Disaster is poised to strike us, and I would be failing in my Christian duty if I did not warn you."

The smile that crept across Belle's face would have astounded those members of the *ton* who had dubbed her "The Golden Icicle." "As you say, Georgiana," she replied, her usually cool voice warm with tolerant affection. "You may consider me warned, and on my head shall the consequences rest."

Suspecting Belle was mocking her, Georgiana gave her a sharp look. "You may scoff if you like, young lady," she said, waggling an admonishing finger, "but if Napoleon had a toe like mine, he'd never have been fool enough to ride into Waterloo."

This was too much even for one with Belle's icy control, and she gave a delighted chuckle. "If Napoleon had your talent, Georgiana, we'd all be speaking French," she said, her golden-brown eyes dancing with laughter. "Now, stop being so gloomy and tell me what you think about my plans for Julia's coming out."

"Rather late to ask *my* opinion of anything, considering the chit is to make her bows tonight,"

Georgiana grumbled, abandoning discussion of her aching ankle with obvious reluctance. "Which reminds me, however were you able to secure a voucher for her? I would have thought Almack's to be quite above her touch."

"Above hers, perhaps, but not above mine." Belle's mild response gave no hint of the effort it had cost her to secure one of the highly prized vouchers. She'd pleaded, bargained, and schemed, but in the end she had triumphed over the patronesses' opposition. Whatever their original objections to admitting a young beauty "two steps removed from the shops" (the countess's exact words), they were too wily to let an heiress like Belle slip through their fingers. Her threat to avoid Almack's if Julia was not admitted had proven most effective, and Belle was cynically amused by the power her fortune commanded.

"Well, it certainly is kind of you to sponsor Julia," Georgiana said. "She is no closer a relation to you than I am."

"Her mother was very kind to mine after my father's death," Belle said, feeling a familiar stab of pain as she remembered those bleak days. "I don't know what would have become of us had Cousin Rachel not paid our passage back from Spain. Certainly no other member of the family seemed inclined to help."

Georgiana glanced away, her rouged cheeks suffusing with color, and Belle was instantly ashamed. Not of what she had said, but because she'd allowed her emotions to show. She'd spent years perfecting her mask of icy indifference, and it distressed her that she'd allowed it to slip even for a moment.

"Speaking of Julia's coming out, it is only six weeks until her ball," she said, hiding her distress behind brisk efficiency. "I'm sure I shall have everything in hand by then, but I would appreciate your going over the final plans. I've never hosted anything so grand, and I would hate to make a foolish mistake."

Before Georgiana could comment, the door to the library opened, and a petite beauty with blond curls floating about her face came scurrying into the room. "I am so sorry to be late, Aunt, Cousin," she said, favoring each lady in turn with an angelic smile, "but Madame Lorraine has only just this moment completed alterations on my ball gown. I trust I didn't keep you waiting overly long?"

"Not at all, dearest," Belle assured her, thinking the apology was a great deal like Julia herself. Sweet, sincere, and graceful. The chit would do well, she decided, with almost maternal pride.

"Madame Lorraine indeed," Georgiana retorted as Julia took her seat. "These mantua-makers like to give themselves French handles so that they can charge the highest prices for their goods, but don't think *I* don't recognize a Yorkshire accent when I hear it. Such duplicity would never have been allowed in my day, I can tell you."

Rather than arguing, Julia merely smiled, her expression sweet as she turned to Belle. "I wish to thank you for the diamonds, Cousin," she said, her thick lashes sweeping over her deep blue eyes. "Simon would insist I not accept them, but I know you only wanted to give me a memento of this evening."

"Thank you, Julia," Belle said, grateful her gesture had been accepted in the spirit in which it was intended. She knew only too well what it was like to be on the receiving end of grudging charity, and she wouldn't have wished to offend either Julia or her stiff-necked elder brother.

"Speaking of Simon, when might we expect to

see the wretch?" Georgiana asked with feigned disinterest. "It is shocking, the way that lad ignores his family."

"He is in the country visiting one of his investments," Julia explained. "He is planning a visit to America to buy cotton for his mills, but he assures me he will be here for my coming-out ball."

Talk of the ball carried them comfortably through the next hour, and as Julia and Georgiana eagerly discussed the merits of various young men of the *ton*, Belle allowed her thoughts to drift to the coming evening. Despite her cool assurances to Georgiana, she couldn't help but feel some trepidation at the thought of introducing Julia to Society. The girl was so sweet, without an ounce of artifice to her, that Belle greatly feared she would be hurt by the sometimes cruel sophistication of the Polite World. Her own wealth could protect the girl only so far, and she knew there were those out there who would already be sharpening their claws in vicious anticipation.

For one moment she was wildly tempted to gather Julia up and rush back to her country estate and safety, but in the next moment her pride reasserted itself. Just let one of those cats attempt to scratch her ward, she vowed, her chin coming up with determination. Julia was her responsibility, and the first person foolish enough to threaten her would soon learn the folly of his actions. If the *ton* thought The Golden Icicle unable or unwilling to protect her own, they were about to learn otherwise.

"Almack's," Mr. Tobias Flanders mumbled in tones of painful resignation. "Really, sir, how can you be so cruel? You must know I'd rather be at m'own hanging than here in this wasp's nest. Couldn't you have come alone?"

"No, I could not," snapped Marcus Wainwright, the earl of Colford, his dark auburn eyebrows meeting over his nose as he cast his heir an impatient look. "Lady Bingington is going to be here tonight, and she hinted she wanted to meet you."

"Don't see why," Toby muttered, his bottom lip thrusting forward in a pout. "You're the one courting the lady, not I."

Marcus's gray eyes frosted over in annoyance. "Toby, might I remind you of what will happen to Colford if I fail to make an advantageous marriage?" he warned, his voice dangerously soft. "I should think that as my heir, you'd want to do everything within your power to insure the estate remains intact."

Rather than bending to his cousin's command, Toby merely looked indifferent. "Wealth," he said in the bored accents of one who had known only privilege and comfort, "such a common preoccupation. As a poet, I am far above such considerations."

Marcus's lips tightened in fury, and he gave careful consideration to tossing his pompous cousin down the Grand Staircase. He could almost see Toby bouncing backside over breakfast down the steps, perhaps bowling over a couple of dowagers in the bargain ... A half smile touched Marcus's mouth at the image, but in the next moment he was reluctantly rejecting it. The lady he was studiously courting was a pattern card of propriety, and he much doubted she would care for the scandal such an action would cause. Toby was safe ... for now.

Thoughts of Charlotte led, as they always did, to thoughts of his estate, for without the one, there was no way he could hang on to the other. Colford was teetering on the edge of destruction, and Marcus knew everything hinged on the coming

Season. He had to make a marriage of convenience, he reminded himself grimly; there was no other choice.

"Almack's." Julia's voice was full of wonder as she glanced wide-eyed about her. "Oh, Cousin, I can scarce believe I am here!"

Belle hid a smile at Julia's expression. "Believe it, my dear," she said, unfurling her fan with practiced grace. "Now, stop gawking, else you risk being taken for a provincial."

"But I *am* a provincial," Julia replied, although she did her best to follow Belle's instructions. "Simon said I should always remember where I came from, so that I won't forget where I must go."

"That sounds like something he would say," Belle agreed with reluctant admiration, "but I would ask you not to repeat it too loudly. I fear there are few here who share Simon's rather interesting view of the world."

The next several minutes were given over to introductions, and Belle was smugly proud of the interest Julia aroused amongst those present. Her fortune and beauty as well as her connection to Belle might have drawn them at first, but it was obvious it was Julia's kindness and charm that made them stay. Watching Julia dazzle one young man after the other, Belle felt a momentary pang of envy as she remembered her own introduction to Society.

Fear had left her so stiff and cold that she'd spent most of the evening in the corner, watching unhappily as others enjoyed themselves. She'd wanted more than anything to join them in their revelry, but years of guarding her emotions from her avaricious relations had left their mark. She could only stand in miserable silence, her face frozen in a haughty mask as her heart ached for an acceptance she could not find.

That night set the pattern for the rest of the Season, and the more people commented on her standoffish behavior, the more she withdrew into an icy shell. Balls and soirees became an agony to be endured until finally she surrendered, stoically accepting the role Society assigned her. By the time the odious earl of Colford christened her The Golden Icicle, her heart was already encased in a cage of frost.

The memory of that occasion still had the power to bring a flash of anger to her eyes. It had been at one of the last balls of the Season, and she'd fled out onto the balcony to escape the crowds and the appalling heat. She'd thought herself quite alone when she turned around to find Lord Colford watching her from the shadows. He'd been only a viscount then, although one would never have guessed it from his arrogance, and that arrogance had been much in evidence as he continued watching her. Finally he pushed himself away from the stone balustrade and advanced lazily toward her, his smile mocking as he gave a low bow.

" 'Well met by moonlight, proud Titania,' " he murmured, his gray eyes resting on her face. "Or should I say, proud Miss Portham? Although you do look so much like a fairy queen in that charming dress, I am sure you can forgive my confusion."

Her heart had raced at the sight of him, a fact she now blushed to recall, and her voice had been none too steady as she returned his greeting. "I thank you for the compliment, my lord, and I shall be sure to extend your appreciation to my modiste."

"You mean the cloth wasn't spun in moonlit glades by elves and sprites?" he drawled, the corners of his lips curving in a wry smile. "You disappoint me, ma'am. How sad to think such a lovely creation came from so prosaic a place as Madame DeClaire's on Bond Street."

That he was aware her gold and white silk gown had been made by Madame gave credence to the whispers she'd heard about his rakish ways, and she decided it might be prudent to return to the ballroom. She muttered a stiff excuse and made to brush past him, but instead of standing aside as a gentleman would have done, he stood his ground, his expression daring her to object.

"Sir, you are in my way," she informed him coolly, ignoring her heart hammering inside her chest. "I will thank you to step aside."

"Will you?" His eyes had glowed silver in the moonlight as he gazed down at her. "And what if I do not? Will you cast one of your spells and turn me into another Oberon?"

"Such a spell would seem superfluous, my lord, as you are already half an ass!" she snapped, and then flushed with mortification. She would have fled at that point but for the powerful hand that curled about her upper arm, staying her.

"One moment, my fairy queen." He laughed, easily controlling her efforts to free herself. "If you think I mean to allow you to leave after that, you are much mistaken. You have insulted me, my sweet, and now you must pay a forfeit."

Before she could scream, his mouth descended on hers, capturing her lips in a kiss of fiery passion. She'd been more furious than frightened at his audacity, sensing somehow that he would never really hurt her. But it was the hateful knowledge that she was actually enjoying the embrace that appalled her most, and the moment her lips were free, she brought her hand across his face in a stinging slap.

"How dare you!" she raged somewhat unoriginally, doing her best to control her agitated breathing. "If you ever touch me again, I vow I shall put a bullet through you!"

"You needn't have any worries on that score, ma'am," he responded sardonically, his hand resting on the red mark her blow had left. "A man would have to be mad to kiss an icicle . . . even a golden one. You have my word I shall keep my distance."

And so he had, she admitted, nodding to a casual acquaintance who was waving at her from across the room. In the eight or so years since that momentous night, she could count on one hand the times they'd exchanged more than a few minutes of brittle conversation. Unfortunately, since he was an intimate of Viscount St. Ives, and she was one of the viscountess's closest friends, she supposed that would change, and she steeled herself for the confrontations that were sure to come.

The next few hours passed pleasantly as Belle introduced Julia to the *ton*. In addition to the eligible men fluttering about her, she also made sure her pretty ward made the acquaintance of several young ladies her own age. She was especially pleased to see Julia strike up a friendship with Lady Katherine Cragswell, the daughter of an old friend. Kate was as good as she was sensible, and it was Belle's hope Julia would learn to emulate the other girl's exquisite manners.

In between keeping a protective eye on Julia and making sure Georgiana lacked for nothing, Belle visited with several of her friends from previous Seasons. But as much as she enjoyed seeing them, she couldn't help but miss her dear friend Phillipa Lambert, now the Viscountess St. Ives. Pip and her handsome husband, Alex, were still in the country at his estates, but the last letter Belle had had from

Pip had hinted they would be coming to London for a visit. She was sharing this bit of news with one of her friends when the lady gave an unexpected giggle.

"It's true, then," she said, her muddy brown eyes sparkling with spite. "I wouldn't have believed it if I hadn't seen it with my own eyes!"

"Believed what?" Belle asked, frowning at Miriam's unseemly behavior. After last year's debacle when the entire *ton* was taking bets as to whether or not Pip and Alex would wed, she had grown overly cautious to gossip of any sort.

"That Lady Bingington has set her cap for the earl of Colford, of course." Miriam gave another high-pitched giggle. "Or rather, it is the other way around. Everyone knows that precious estate of his is all but bankrupt, and he must make a marriage of convenience if he hopes to save it."

Even though she considered the earl her enemy, Belle was not about to stand idly by while his good name was besmirched. Drawing herself up, she fixed Miriam with her haughtiest stare. "I should take care not to repeat such tattle, Miriam," she said coolly. "In the event it turns out to be a lie, you risk looking the fool."

"Belle!" Miriam exclaimed, her angular face turning an unbecoming shade of red. "I never thought to hear you speak so to me! I thought we were friends."

"And so we are," Belle replied, her voice not warming by a single degree. "But you must know I do not countenance gossip. It is ill bred in the extreme, and I for one do not choose to listen to it. In the future I would thank you to remember that."

"But you don't even like Colford!"

"Perhaps not," Belle said, inclining her head regally, "but I dislike more listening to his name being bandied about when he is not present to defend himself. Now, if you will excuse me, I must go and check on my cousin." And with that, she walked away, her back rigid with displeasure.

Across the room, Marcus watched the exchange with interest. He'd seen Miss Portham and her ward arrive several hours ago, and as usual, Miss Portham's stunning beauty had made his breath catch. Dressed in a gown of sapphire silk, her dark blond hair swept in a sophisticated chignon, she was a sight to give any man pause. She was standing off to one side, affording him a glimpse of her exquisite profile, and his eyes lingered on the curve of her high cheekbones and the tempting bow of her full lips.

A pity such loveliness was wrapped in impenetrable ice, he thought, recalling the one time he'd attempted to melt that ice and had all but been frozen to death for his pains. The thought of repeating the incident was tempting, and he knew a flash of disappointment that he would never have that chance. If all went as he planned, he would soon be a married man, and unlike his father, he had no intention of ever breaking his sacred vows.

"You are rather quiet this evening, my lord," Lady Charlotte Bingingham, the widow of the duke of Bingingham, observed softly, laying a solicitous hand on his arm. "Is everything all right?"

Marcus turned his back on Miss Portham, focusing his attention on Charlotte. "I was but thinking how depressingly young this year's crop of debs looks," he said, lowering his deep voice to its most attractive level. "The thought of dancing with one is almost indecent."

This was a sentiment that was music to Charlotte's thirty-one-year-old ears. "I can see your point, my lord," she replied, a pleased smile playing about her full lips. "I recall thinking much the same thing last year when George's youngest boy, Harry, was trotted out. I also recall uttering a silent prayer of relief that all of this is finally behind me. Being a widow does have its advantages, thank God."

Her candidness was one of the things Marcus most liked about Charlotte. Her marriage to a man almost thirty years her senior had been arranged, and she had never pretended otherwise. Even though it wasn't a love match, she had obviously liked and respected her elderly husband, and she'd done her best to be a stepmama to his already grown sons. She'd also been a faithful wife, something Marcus had taken discreet pains to learn. Desperate though he was to make a suitable marriage, he wasn't about to offer his name to a lady who would only shame it.

"Speaking of Harry, how is the lad doing?" he asked, knowing Charlotte was devoted to her stepsons. "Did he buy that bay he was considering?"

"No." Charlotte gave a warm chuckle. "I did as you suggested and mentioned how happy I was he was buying the animal so that I could borrow it. The notion of owning a horse his stepmama coveted was enough to put him off the nag altogether, thank heavens. He'd have broken his neck on the wretched beast inside of a week."

"I had a similar feeling about a bit of blood Toby was eyeing," Marcus said, his gray eyes searching the room for his heir. The dolt had wandered off a few minutes ago, and now there was no sign of him.

"How were you able to dissuade him?"

There he was, standing by The Icicle and her ward. Marcus raised a commanding eyebrow. "By pointing out the horse made him look like a fat child riding an undersized pony," he replied, frowning as Toby remained where he was. "He didn't think the image proper for a Corinthian."

Charlotte smiled in appreciation of Colford's guile. "Your heir fancies himself a Corinthian, does he?"

"That was last year. This year the fool thinks he's Byron," Marcus muttered, realizing that if he wished for Toby to meet Lady Bingingham, he'd have to fetch him himself. He turned to the duchess with an apologetic smile.

"Speaking of our budding poet, I can see him standing over there worshiping at the feet of his latest muse. With your permission, I will go and pry him free. I'll only be a moment." And he stalked off before Lady Bingingham could stop him.

". . . not spun gold; dashed cliché, that," Toby was saying as Marcus walked up behind him. "Besides, when was the last time anyone saw spun gold, I should like to know. No, I should liken your hair to sunlight, or yellow roses; fragile and lovely. I—"

"Toby!"

"What?" Toby gave a leap and whirled around, his look of alarm fading as he saw his elder cousin standing there. "I say, Colford, you did give me a start," he said, laying his hand over his wildly racing heart. "What the devil do you mean sneaking up on people like that? Dashed inconsiderate, if you ask me."

"Almost as inconsiderate as keeping a lady waiting," Marcus said, his anger hardly soothed by the look of cool annoyance he received from Miss Portham. "Lady Bingingham is waiting to make your acquaintance."

"Oh, is that why you was waggling your eyebrows at me?" Toby asked, turning back to the ladies. "My cousin is thinking of marrying her ladyship," he confided with a conspiratorial smile. "He wants her to meet me so she'll know there ain't no boobies in the family."

"If I wanted her ladyship to think that, then I would take very great care to see the two of you never met," Marcus retorted between clenched teeth. He knew the remark to be unkind in the extreme, but he'd been unable to help himself. There were times when Toby was so hopelessly thick, it would have taken a saint to have borne him, and a saint was something Marcus had never claimed to be.

"That was irony," Toby explained to the blonde. "I recognize it. It's a literary device Byron sometimes uses, but I—"

"*Tobias!*"

"Oh, very well." Toby sighed, capturing the girl's hand in his. "But first let me make you known to Miss Julia Dolitan. Miss Dolitan, this is m'cousin, Lord Marcus Wainwright, earl of Colford. Miss Dolitan is The Icicle's ward, Colford."

Toby's incautious use of Miss Portham's nickname in front of her made Marcus wince, and he vowed to have yet another word with him on the need for discretion. "Miss Dolitan"—he gave the young woman a stiff bow—"it is a pleasure to meet you. And Miss Portham, I am delighted to see you once more."

"Yes, I can see that you are," Belle drawled, amused at his discomfiture. It was obvious he found his dense heir a trial, and she took malicious pleasure in the knowledge. Good, she thought smugly, it served the arrogant devil right.

Marcus stiffened at the mocking note in her voice and the calculating sparkle in her gold-colored eyes. Why the devil was he fretting about her tender feelings? he wondered with a flash of

irritation. It was obvious she had none. She was
every bit the icicle he'd named her, and for a moment he was strongly tempted to tell her so. Unfortunately such an action would create a certain
scandal and put an end to any hopes he had of
winning the duchess. Swallowing his anger, he
managed a cool smile.

"If you ladies will forgive me for being rude, I
must introduce Toby to Lady Bingingham. She
stopped by on her way to another party, but she is
in something of a hurry." And without further cer-
emony, he dragged his heir off to meet the lady he
hoped to make his bride.

"That went rather well, don't you think?"
Georgiana asked, settling back with a sigh as their
carriage pulled away from Almack's. "Didn't
think it would, but it did."

"Of course it did," Belle said, exchanging a wink
with Julia. "I told you I had everything well in
hand."

"Maybe. But you know what the Holy Scrip-
tures have to say about pride," the older woman
retorted, unwilling to discount her throbbing ankle
without a fight. "And we ain't safely home yet,
you know. We could always be attacked by foot-
pads."

" 'Hope springs eternal,' " Belle obliged, quoting
Pope with a rare grin. The night *had* gone well, she
thought, relief making her giddy. Much as she
would rather die than admit it, she had been just
the triflest bit uneasy. Georgiana's twinges did
have an uncanny habit of preceding some calami-
tous event, and she'd been holding her breath in
dreadful anticipation of some disaster striking the
moment she dropped her guard. That they had
survived the night intact was indeed an encouraging sign.

"And what are your thoughts of this evening, dearest?" she asked, shifting in her seat to study Julia's face. "Was Almack's everything you expected?"

"I suppose." To Belle's surprise, Julia gave an uninterested shrug. "I thought most of the people rather flat and full of themselves . . . except for Mr. Flanders, that is."

Belle, who had been about to congratulate her ward on her acuity, gazed at her in alarm. "Mr. Flanders?" she echoed, praying she'd misheard.

"The earl of Colford's heir," Julia provided, unaware of the effect her dreamy smile was having upon her mentor. "He is a poet, you know, and a most worthy gentleman. I quite liked him."

This couldn't be happening, Belle thought with growing horror. Of all the catastrophes she'd envisioned, she had never considered anything so vile as her ward becoming enamored of a member of Colford's family. She remembered Georgiana's prophetic ankle and bit back a hysterical laugh. Georgiana had merely said the wretched thing ached, she thought. If Julia *was* in love with Flanders, the wretched thing would have throbbed with agony.

"Colford's heir?" Georgiana was frowning in consideration. "He's not too bad, I suppose. Bit of a dolt, but I've always said it never does for a man to be too clever. I wouldn't count on his ever inheriting, though. Colford's young yet and will probably sire half a dozen sons before cocking up his toes."

"Oh, Tobias knows the title will never be his." Julia dismissed this objection with a laugh. "He says he doesn't want the bloody thing, and I must say I admire him the more for it."

"Julia!"

"Well, I do." Julia gave Belle an apologetic look.

"As for my saying 'bloody,' I know I shouldn't have, but I was merely quoting Tobias. He says it all the time."

"All the time?" Belle wondered if she would have to lower herself to ask for Georgiana's smelling salts. "Do you mean to say you have met Mr. Flanders before now?"

"Of course not," Julia denied with a pretty laugh. "No, I merely meant that from the way he said it, I could tell it was a favorite expression of his. He apologized, of course, but I told him not to mind. You ought to hear some of the things Simon mutters."

"I can imagine," Belle said weakly, several pithy phrases occurring to her as she struggled for calm. "Julia, you can not *really* like Mr. Flanders," she said, deciding cool logic was the best approach. "Granted he is ... er ... a very handsome man, and it is not beyond credulity that you would be taken by him, but I assure you it is nothing more."

"You think Tobias handsome?" Julia sounded surprised. "How odd. I first thought him a plump, prosy bore." She sighed again. "At least until I saw his eyes. He has quite the loveliest eyes I've ever seen, as brown and rich as mahogany. And when I learned he was a poet, I knew I had misjudged him."

Hearing the note of girlish admiration in her voice, Belle wished she'd lowered her pride to ask for the smelling salts. She'd never felt more like swooning in her life, and the only thing that kept her from succumbing was the knowledge that she had to save her ward from the magnitude of her folly.

The carriage was slowing, and a quick glance out the window showed they were pulling to a halt in front of her home on Harrow Square. Clearly it was too late to do anything tonight, she decided, but first thing tomorrow morning, she meant to get started at once. There was no way on this earth she would allow any member of her family to enter into an alliance with that man's family. Colford might be an earl, but she herself was not without influence. If it came to daggers drawn, they would just see who emerged the victor.

Marcus spent the next morning holed up in his office as he went over his accounts. Selling off the last of his hunters had raised enough to pay his taxes, so he no longer had that threat hanging over his head. Now if he could just raise another five thousand pounds or so, he might make it through the next year without having to sell the clothes from his back, he thought, his mouth twisting in a bitter smile.

He was studying some ideas for investments he'd received that morning when Toby wandered in, his cravat lying half-tied about his throat. "I need a word that rhymes with rose," he said, throwing himself into the chair facing Marcus's desk. "Can't think of anything but toes, and it don't seem proper using such a word in a love poem."

"Toby, can't you see that I'm busy?" Marcus asked, cursing the necessity of having Toby live with him rather than putting him up in his own lodgings. "Go compose somewhere else."

" 'Compose'; that rhymes with rose." Toby hurriedly scratched it down. "Thank you, Colford. Anything else?"

"No, but if you don't leave this instant, they'll have to find a word to rhyme with 'strangled' when they carve your epitaph!"

" 'Mangled' might work," Toby suggested, laying a blunt finger on his lips. "Or 'dangled.' That would suggest hanging, and—"

"Toby," Marcus interrupted, squeezing his eyes shut and pinching the bridge of his nose, "I should hate the necessity of murdering you, but if you don't take yourself off, I am afraid you will leave me no other choice."

Toby hauled himself to his feet, his fleshy features assuming a look of outraged dignity. "There is no need to act the bully with me, sir," he said haughtily. "I only stopped by to wish you good morning. My apologies if I have disturbed you."

Marcus thrust an impatient hand through his auburn hair and uttered a curse beneath his breath. Damned if the young puppy didn't make him feel guilty, he thought, eyeing Toby's retreating form with resignation. And the devil of it was, he was right. He had no right to take his frustrations out on the other man.

"Toby, wait."

"Yes?" Toby paused with his hand on the doorknob.

"It is I who ought to be apologizing," Marcus admitted, rising to his feet. "I was wrong to snap at you like that, and I hope you will forgive me for my churlish behavior."

Toby hesitated, unwilling to give up his role of the persecuted artist, but in the end his own good nature won the day. "Certainly, my lord," he said, savoring the taste of magnanimity. "As a poet, I quite understand black moods and all that. No harm done, eh?"

"If you say so." Marcus was still feeling slightly ashamed. "Was there anything else you wished?"

"Well, now that you mention it, there *is* one favor I should like to ask of you," Toby admitted, sending Marcus a hopeful look. "I was to ride out with Cleves Barrowby this morning, but he had to cancel. Don't suppose you'd like to go with me?"

Marcus glanced down at the papers spread out

on his desk. He'd planned to spend the rest of the morning going over them and arranging payment, but he imagined it wouldn't hurt if he was to put the task off for another day. Reaching a swift decision, he raised his eyes to Toby. "A morning ride sounds just the thing," he said, dredging up an enthusiastic smile. "Only give me a half hour or so to change, and I shall meet you in the foyer."

Some forty minutes later, Marcus and Toby were on their mounts and cantering toward Hyde Park. In an effort to trim costs he had eliminated his London stable, and was forced to board his horses in a public stable. He knew it would prove even cheaper to hire horses as needed, but there were some economies he was still unwilling to make. Not just for appearance' sake, he admitted, reaching down to give his horse's neck a fond pat, but because he loved a good ride. Considering all the other pleasures he'd been forced to give up, he wasn't about to sacrifice his beloved horses as well.

Although it was fairly early in the day, the park was already filled with riders, and both Marcus and Toby exchanged greetings with several friends. They'd just made their first circuit about Rotten Row when Toby suddenly pulled his horse to a halt. " 'It is the east, and Julia is the sun,' " he murmured, one gloved hand going to his heart.

Marcus gave him an amused look and was about to correct him when he followed the direction of Toby's stare. "I believe the lady's name was Juliet," he said, a sardonic grin spreading across his face. "But seeing Miss Dolitan, I can see how one could become confused. She is lovely, is she not?"

"Lovely?" Toby dismissed the paltry word with a snort. "She is beautiful, a vision, a goddess. She . . ." He ran out of superlatives and contented himself with a sigh. "She is wonderful," he concluded, his heart in his eyes as he gazed at his lady fair like a besotted knight of old.

"Indeed." Marcus was only mildly intrigued by his heir's passionate declaration. In the few weeks they'd been back in London, Toby had fallen in love at least three times by Marcus's reckoning, and he surmised that like those "deathless loves," this infatuation would also quickly die. Although he had no great objections if it did not. For once, the object of Toby's poetic heart was actually well dowered.

"Gad, she sees us!" Toby gave a yelp of alarm as Miss Dolitan raised her whip in greeting. "What shall we do?"

"Return her greeting, if you count yourself a gentleman," Marcus answered, already tipping his hat in acknowledgment. His eyes strayed past Miss Dolitan to rest on her companion, and a slow, wicked smile spread across his face. Miss Portham was sitting atop a magnificent black, her slender body displayed to best advantage in a habit of mulberry velvet. Her famous blond tresses were topped by a jaunty black hat, and if the frozen look on her face was any indication, she was less than thrilled with the chance encounter. He supposed a gentleman would honor her unspoken preference and continue on his way, but as he'd never paid much mind to such dicta, he saw no reason why he should start now.

"Well, what are you waiting for, slow top?" he drawled, an imp of mischief making his eyes gleam with laughter. "As you are so fond of poetical sayings, you ought to know that tide and time wait for no man. Come." And he nudged his horse forward, leaving Toby no choice but to follow.

Two

Across the green expanse Julia watched their approach with awe-filled eyes. "They are coming over!" she cried, her hands tightening on the reins and causing her small bay to dance in protest. "Oh dearest Belle, whatever shall we do?"

"Perhaps that is something you ought to have considered before drawing their notice," Belle suggested coolly, her anger directed more at Colford than at her green cousin. She'd seen the devilish glint in his silver eyes, and knew he'd deliberately sought them out to vex her. Well—her chin came up with the cold pride that had sustained her over the last dozen years—she was cursed if she'd oblige him.

"Is he not splendid on horseback?" Julia was saying, her eyes dreamy as she watched the approaching men. "He reminds me of one of those dashing corsairs Byron writes about."

Belle's eyes rested on Toby's unremarkable form bouncing up and down on the gray he was riding, and she decided humorously that if infatuation wasn't blind, it was at the very least nearsighted. Now, if it were Colford Julia was mooning over, she supposed she might have better understood the analogy. However much she might dislike the

wretch, there was no denying he was an arresting
sight on horseback.

Dressed in a riding jacket of hunter green that
made his hair gleam like polished copper, he stood
out amongst the fops and Corinthians of Hyde
Park like a tiger in a litter of tabby cats. His deeply
tanned features were perhaps a trifle too harsh to
fit in the classically handsome mold made so pop-
ular by Byron and the others, but she could grudg-
ingly find no fault in his sharp blade of a nose and
firmly molded jaw. Even his physique went
against fashion, hard and muscular when slender,
aesthetic forms were all the rage, and she knew
from experience that his broad shoulders owed little to his tailor's art. When he'd pulled her into his
arms and kissed her, it had taken every ounce of
strength she'd possessed to fight her way free . . .

As she realized the direction of her thoughts,
Belle's lips tightened in fury. Every time she
thought of the insulting embrace he'd forced upon
her, the more she enjoyed the memory of slapping
his arrogant face. It had been the crowning humil-
iation of her disastrous first Season, and if it was
the last thing she did she vowed she'd repay him
for the painful recollection.

None of these dark thoughts were evident in the
coolly polite mask she assumed as the gentlemen
joined them. Indeed, her manner was everything it
ought to be as she inclined her head in a greeting.
"My lord, Mr. Flanders," she said as they pulled
their mounts to a halt, "a lovely day for a ride, is
it not?"

"Quite lovely, Miss Portham," Marcus responded, his lips twitching at her starchy tones.
Then, knowing it would further annoy her, he
added, "Almost as lovely as you and your charming ward."

The flash of fire in her golden eyes did not disappoint him. "Your lordship is very practiced with his flattery," Belle said, detesting him for his ability to shake her icy control. She knew he was baiting her, and hated that she seemed helpless to resist responding. Clearly it was time to move on. She turned to Julia to suggest they return home only to find her and Mr. Flanders exchanging languishing looks.

"You are a vision, Miss Dolitan." Toby's voice was worshipful as he gazed at his beloved. "With your permission, I should very much like to dedicate my next poem to you."

"Oh, sir!" Julia's dimpled cheeks bloomed with rose. "I should like that above all things."

"Julia," Belle began, thoroughly alarmed, "I do not think it proper you should be party to such a thing. The tattle—"

Marcus leaned forward in his saddle to lay a comforting hand over hers. "Relax, Miss Portham," he advised in a low voice that scarcely reached her ears. "I have had the misfortune of reading one of Toby's efforts, and you may rest assured there is little chance of their ever being seen . . . let alone published."

"That is not the point, sir," Belle protested. "Julia is my ward, and it is my duty to protect her!"

"And Toby, to my grief, is my heir. It is my responsibility to see he comes to no harm," Marcus returned coldly, his gray eyes challenging hers. "Do you mean to imply I am less attentive in my duty than you are in yours?"

The words as well as the haughty tone in which they were delivered brought a faint flush of shame to Belle's cheeks. "Of course not," she denied, her eyes dropping to her hands. "But a young girl's reputation if far more fragile than that of a man. If word of this silly poem should leak out—"

"It won't," he interrupted, enjoying the novel sight of Miss Portham nonplussed. "Whatever Toby's other faults, he does have the sense not to force his scribblings on others. But if it will reassure you, I promise to have a word with him. Does that make you feel better?"

Oddly enough, it did, and Belle gave him a sheepish smile. "I would be grateful if you would, my lord," she said, her voice rueful as she met his gaze. "I know I am probably being overprotective, but I did promise Simon I would have a care of his sister, and I should hate to fail him."

"Simon?"

"Miss Dolitan's older brother. He was against my introducing Julia to Society, and it was only by promising I would allow no harm to befall her that I was able to win his consent."

"Why should he oppose his sister being introduced?" Marcus asked, his eyes straying to Miss Dolitan, who was engaged in her own conversation with Toby. Her habit was of sapphire velvet, and with her blond hair and dark blue eyes, she was fetching. He would have thought any brother—particularly one involved in trade, as he knew Miss Dolitan's brother to be—would be delighted at having his sister offered such an opportunity.

Belle's smile grew warm at the thought of Simon's intractable pride. "I fear Simon has little opinion of our world," she said, unaware of the affection that was evident in her soft tones. "He is forever lecturing me on the superficiality of the *ton*, and demanding I return to the country."

Marcus's dark eyebrows arched at this confession. "Indeed?" he drawled, impressed anyone would dare lecture to The Golden Icicle. "As you are here, I presume you declined to follow his sage advice?"

"I told him to mind his own business and to stop being so high in the instep," Belle confessed with a chuckle as she recalled their heated exchange. "But in the end I was able to persuade him to give Julia these few months with me, and I am determined to see she uses them well."

As the object of any Season was an advantageous marriage, Marcus couldn't help but wonder if that was Miss Portham's plan for her ward. If so, then perhaps it wouldn't hurt to begin mending his fences with her. If the gossip he'd heard was any indication, the girl was as well dowered as she was lovely, and he could see no reason why Toby shouldn't court her. The Lord knew they could use the blunt, he admitted with a cynical twist of his lips. All that remained now was determining her intentions.

"If Miss Dolitan's brother is so opposed to a London Season, then how would he react to her making a Society marriage?" he asked, pretending only polite interest. "Will he cut her out of his life in a suitably dramatic fashion?"

"Simon?" Belle gave a tinkling laugh as she considered such an impossibility. "Heavens, no! He adores Julia, and so long as her husband loves her, I am sure he would have no objections."

"Love?" Marcus's hopes for a quick match faltered.

"Love," Belle repeated, amused by his expression. "An odd basis for a marriage in our world, I grant you, but it is the only reason Simon would ever accept. If he even suspected a man of courting Julia for her fortune, I fear he would take drastic and decided action."

"So it will be pistols at dawn then, eh?" Marcus asked, wondering what action he should take if Toby's passion proved lasting.

"As Simon is not a member of the *ton*, I much

doubt his challenge would be accepted," Belle said with a sagacious laugh. "More like he would beat the poor devil within an inch of his life, and then send him on his way with a flea in his ear."

Marcus looked at Toby. "Oh."

The ride continued in silence, and while Belle wondered if she ought to make some effort to separate Julia from Mr. Flanders, Marcus was hastily reviewing his options. He knew that in the event Toby's infatuation faded—as it surely would—there was no way his doltish cousin could pretend to be in love with Miss Dolitan ... however rewarding such a deception might prove. He spared a few seconds to mourn the loss of the badly needed dowry she might have brought with her, and then decided to put an end to the puppy's ardent pursuit. However much Toby might annoy him, he really had no desire to see him hurt.

"I meant to ask you, my lord, if you have heard from Lord St. Ives" Belle asked when she'd grown weary of the silence. "I had a note from Pip last week, and she mentioned they would be returning to the city within the week."

"Yes," Marcus answered, shaking off his glum thoughts. "Alex is returning for the session on the new Trade Acts, and I am looking forward to debating him."

"Are you?" Belle stirred with sudden interest, for she was quite interested in politics. Last year she'd even considered marrying Lord St. Ives so that she could obtain power as his political hostess, but the viscount had fallen in love with Pip instead, and after a riotous courtship which had kept all of London agog, they had married.

"You sound surprised," Marcus said in answer to her remark. "Do you think me so indifferent to my duties as a member of the House of Lords?"

"Of course not, sir," she denied, striving for indifference. "I was but expressing surprise that one Tory would waste his breath arguing against another."

Her response drew a low chuckle from him. "Yes, I'd forgotten you were afflicted with Whiggish sympathies," he said, slanting her a teasing grin. "But never fear, ma'am, I shan't hold your failings against you."

"Your lordship is too kind." Belle's melodic voice dripped with polite sarcasm.

"Not at all. But in response to your earlier remark, I will be debating against the proposed sanctions while St. Ives will be arguing in favor of them. Just because we are friends and fellow Tories doesn't mean we cannot possess differing opinions."

Belle was much struck by his remark. She and Pip had disagreed as often as they agreed, and their friendship remained firm. That this was also true of his lordship and St. Ives pleased her, for she recalled the heated and often bitter quarrels that had divided her uncles. She was brooding over her dark memories when she heard someone calling her name, and she glanced up to see a man on horseback galloping toward them.

"Miss Portham, I thought that was you!" Stephen Fraiser, the marquess of Berwick, greeted her with a charming smile, lifting his hat to her as he bowed in his saddle. "How long have you been back in London?"

"A few weeks, my lord," Belle answered, her social mask sliding easily into place. She'd met the marquess at several political meetings last year, and she thought him rather nice in a vague way.

"You're here for the debates, I'll wager." The marquess gave a rich chuckle. "If so, I should be happy to provide a pass to the visitors' gallery. I know how much you like politics."

He made her sound like a girl who was overly fond of bonbons, Belle thought sourly, her back stiffening at the condescension in his deep voice. "That is very good of you, sir," she began in her most dampening manner, "but—"

"But she has just accepted a pass from me," Marcus concluded, sending the other man a smile of masculine triumph. "Will you be debating, Berwick?"

Berwick's hazel eyes took on a sudden chill. "I had planned to, yes," he answered evenly. "And you?"

"Most assuredly. In fact, Miss Portham and I were just discussing the matter when you joined us. Tell me, my lord, are you for or against the trade sanctions being proposed?"

Berwick gave him a look that was fairly dripping with animosity. "I have not yet decided," he said, his tone curt. "Now, if you will excuse me, I see a friend ahead of me. Miss Portham, Colford." He wheeled his horse around and departed without another word.

An awkward silence followed, and it was a few seconds before Belle spoke. "There was no need for you to tell his lordship a clapper," she said, her eyes meeting his in cool disapproval. "I am more than capable of handling unwanted offers."

Marcus's jaw dropped at having his gallantry tossed back in his face. Granted his original motive for telling the lie was a desire to discomfit Berwick, but he'd also wanted to spare Miss Portham from embarrassment. And this was his thanks. Well, the devil with her, he decided, drawing himself up proudly.

"Of that, Miss Portham, I make no doubt," he said, every inch the offended earl. "In the future might I suggest you learn to discern a friendly offer from an unfriendly one before you so graciously decline both? Toby!" He called out to his cousin, who was still engaged in intense conversation with Miss Dolitan. "It is time to go."

"Now?" Toby looked crestfallen. "But—"

"Now," Marcus repeated firmly, his hands tightening on the reins. "We have imposed upon the ladies long enough."

Whatever his reluctance to be parted from his ladylove, Toby knew better than to argue when Colford's voice took on that hard edge. Turning to Miss Dolitan, he availed himself of her tiny hand and carried it to his lips. "The minutes will be as hours," he informed her, pitching his voice low. "Say you will be thinking of me."

Julia's cheeks bloomed with delight. "I . . . I suppose that might be arranged, sir," she said, keeping her eyes demurely cast down. Secretly she was thrilled, and couldn't wait to get home so that she could note the incident in her journal. It was just like the novels Miriam Westwood used to smuggle into the school, she thought, casting Toby a languishing look beneath her thick lashes. All that was required was parental disapproval, and their romance would be complete.

The Captain Portham Academy was located on a small back street far removed from the refined elegance of Mayfair. Glancing up at the sparkling windows and rosy bricks, Belle felt a swell of pride. The school for the orphaned children of England's gallant soldiers had long been a dream of hers, and she could still scarce believe it was a reality. Instructing her coachman to return in two hours, she gathered up her books and baskets and hurried inside.

The headmistress, Mrs. Langston, was hard at work in her study, but upon hearing of Belle's arrival, she hurried into the hall to greet her. "Miss

Portham, what a pleasure to see you again!" she
exclaimed, taking Belle's hand with a ready smile.
"I hope all is well with you?"

"Quite well, Mrs. Langston, thank you," Belle
answered, her light brown eyes sparkling with affection as she gazed at the diminutive woman. "I
have brought some books for your older students," she said, indicating the basket at her feet,
"and I was hoping you might let me peek in on a
class while I am here."

"We would be delighted," Mrs. Langston assured her, thinking what a sweet creature her benefactress was. Those Society folk who labeled her
as cold didn't know what they were saying, she
decided, her expression thoughtful as she led the
way to the classrooms located in the rear of the old
house.

The first classroom they peeked into was for the
younger children, and Belle spent several minutes
listening to the lessons and then visiting with the
small students. Those who knew her from previous visits knew she always carried sweetmeats in
her pocket, and several small hands crept into her
pocket, helping themselves to the unexpected
treat. Only one girl hung back, her violet-colored
eyes wary.

"And who might you be, my dear?" Belle asked,
realizing the child was a recent addition. "I am
Miss Portham."

The little girl gave a solemn nod. "I know," she
said, her wispy voice scarcely reaching Belle's
ears. "I heard the others talk about you."

"Then you have the advantage on me," Belle
said. There was something about the girl that
touched her deep inside. "Will you not tell me
who you are?"

The teacher, flushing at her student's slowness
in responding, stepped forward to provide her

name, but Belle waved her back. The little girl hesitated, then raised her small chin with a gesture of pride that pulled at Belle's heart. "I am Miss Amanda Perryvale," she said, her odd-colored eyes meeting Belle's with surprising maturity. "My papa was the youngest son of the duke of Tilton, and he was the bravest soldier that ever was."

"Indeed," Belle replied, wondering why the child was in their care when she was obviously so well connected. "My papa was a soldier, too. Did you know that?"

Again the little girl nodded. "He was killed in Spain," she provided, inching closer. "I heard Miss Pringle telling Miss Marston he was a captain. My papa was a colonel."

"Ah." Belle gave a solemn nod, understanding the child's desperate pride in her deceased father. "Then he must have been a very good soldier indeed."

Amanda's bottom lip trembled. "He was. My grandfather says I don't remember him, but I do remember. I *do*."

The defiance in that quavering voice was Belle's undoing. Without giving the matter another thought, she gathered the small girl against her, her hands gentle as she smoothed the blond hair from her flushed cheeks. "I know you do, dearest," she said softly, her own eyes misting as she gazed down into her face. "Your memories of your papa are the dearest things you have. Don't let anyone take them from you. All right?"

Amanda gave a loud sniff. "All right," she said, rubbing her eyes with a fist. "Can I have some candy, too?"

"Of course you may," Belle replied, blinking back tears as she handed the child a piece of wrapped chocolate. "There you are. Now, be a good girl and go back and join the others."

Later as she and Mrs. Langston sat in her study sharing a cup of tea, Belle asked her information on the little girl.

"Such a sad story, really," the older woman provided with a shake of her head. "Her mother was the daughter of her father's regimental sergeant, and he married her quite against his family's wishes. He fell at New Orleans when Amanda was scarce three, and his family disavowed any responsibility for them. They were living with her mother's aunt until eight weeks ago when her mother died in a carriage accident, and Amanda was eventually brought here."

Belle said nothing. Mrs. Langston was right, she thought, battling down the old hurts and resentments; it was a sad story. Moreover it was a story she knew all too well. Her father's relations had never forgiven her mother for marrying their precious son, and after his death, they never missed an opportunity to show that disapproval to her and her mother. They were shifted from home to home, tolerated but never welcomed by the family that preached charity even as it practiced spite. Just as things were looking their bleakest, a distant great-aunt passed away, leaving Belle the sole heiress to half a million pounds, and she and her mother were catapulted from near poverty to undreamed-of wealth. *Then* they were welcomed, she thought bitterly, remembering the custody battles that ensued following her mother's untimely death. At the age of twelve she learned her only value lay in her fortune, and it was a lesson she was determined never to forget.

"I had thought of writing the duke," Mrs. Langston continued in a thoughtful tone, "but I wasn't sure how you would feel. His Grace is said to be quite powerful, and it may not do to cross him. The gentry can be odd about such things, you know."

"Indeed I do, Mrs. Langston," Belle answered grimly. "For the moment I think it might be best if we did nothing. Besides, children like Amanda are the reason I founded this school. She will be safe with us, I assure you."

"Do you think so?" The schoolmistress looked relieved. "I must own I was of two minds what I should do, and Thomasina was all for storming over to Belgravia and bearding the lion ... er ... the duke in his den. I made her promise to wait until I had consulted you."

"Thomasina?" The name was not familiar to Belle.

"Thomasina Pringle, the newest member of our staff," Mrs. Langston provided. "She is also the daughter of a fallen soldier, and I felt that would give her a better understanding of our pupils. She is a gifted teacher, but there are times when she is a trifle headstrong. Nothing *revolutionary*, mind, but once she gets a notion in her head, I fear there is no stopping her."

That sounded most intriguing to Belle, and had time allowed, she would have enjoyed making the other woman's acquaintance. Unfortunately it was already past one o'clock, and she was due at a lecture by two. Making a mental note to introduce herself to the redoubtable Miss Pringle at the first opportunity, she rose to her feet, leaving Mrs. Langston with a smile and a bank draft that had the other lady stuttering her thanks.

Outside, she was vexed to find no sight of either her carriage or her coachman. Since it was unlike Jackson to be late, she decided he must have been unavoidably detained, and that left her no choice but to flag down a hackney. Since there were none to be seen on the small side street, she began making her way toward the next street, where she was certain she would have no trouble in securing transportation. She'd just reached the curb when a carriage pulled up beside her, and the occupant lowered the window to greet her.

"Miss Portham, is that you?"

Belle's eyes widened as she recognized Lord Berwick. "Indeed it is, my lord," she said coolly, wondering what had brought him to this isolated corner of St. John's Wood.

"But what are you doing here without proper escort?" The earl sounded scandalized as he climbed down from the carriage to confront her. "Is everything all right?"

"Certainly, sir," Belle assured him, bristling at the note of censure in his voice. "I was but walking over to the next street to hire a carriage. My coachman has been delayed and I—"

"Then you must take mine," Lord Berwick interrupted. "I can easily hire another one."

Belle hesitated, knowing the sensible thing would be to accept his kind offer. Still, she hated taking anything from anyone. "That is very good of your lordship," she began in her coolest tones, "but I really couldn't impose upon you."

"No, no, I insist," the earl replied, his expression earnest as she gazed down into her wary eyes. "What sort of gentleman would I be to leave a lady in distress without protection?"

His pompous manner was beginning to grate on Belle's nerves. "I am hardly at the mercy of dragons, sir," she chided, thinking he was making much ado about nothing.

"Worse, you are at the mercy of the London streets," Berwick corrected, still looking stern. "And that is something I cannot allow. Please take my carriage."

Belle did not see how she could refuse. "Very

well, Lord Berwick," she said, giving in with a good-natured smile. "It is most kind of you."

"Not at all, Miss Portham," he said, helping her into the carriage. "The pleasure is mine. In these modern times it's not often a man is granted the opportunity to act as knight errant for a lady fair."

His repartee delighted Belle, and she cautiously revised her earlier opinion of him. "In which case, Sir Knight, I would ask that you allow me to repay you for your gallant act," she said, allowing her guard to drop as she held out her hand to him. "I am holding a small tea Thursday next, and I would be pleased if you would attend."

Berwick accepted her hand with a courtly bow. "I should be honored to do so, milady," he said, his hazel eyes meeting hers. "And might I hope you will save me a dance at the Merricks' soiree? You are attending?" he asked when she hesitated.

"Yes," she admitted, hoping he didn't think she was snubbing him, "but I hadn't planned on dancing. I usually sit with the older ladies and gossip. But I suppose I might make an exception this one time," she added at the disappointed look that flashed across his handsome features.

The look cleared as if by magic, and he favored her with a dazzling smile. "I shall look forward to it," he said, stepping back from the carriage and signaling the driver to continue. "Until then, Miss Portham, I shall bid you adieu."

Jackson returned to the house several hours later, his beefy face bright with consternation as he stood before Belle. "I don't know what happened, Miss Portham," he said, twisting his hat between his hands. "I was at the Bull and Dog having my wee pint, and when I come out, the reins had all been cut. I fixed 'em quick as I could, but when I got to the school, you was gone." He lowered his eyes. "I'll clear my things out of the stables."

"Nonsense, Jackson," Belle responded, her expression softening as she studied him. "You are an excellent driver, and I'm not about to dispense with your services because of something which was clearly beyond your control."

"Then you won't be giving me the sack?"

"Certainly not!" She gave him an indignant look. "Someone cutting the traces is hardly *your* fault. Doubtlessly it was one of those tiresome Corinthians playing a trick on you. It sounds the harebrained sort of stunt one of them would pull."

"Thank you, miss." Jackson cleared his throat and shifted awkwardly from one foot to the other. "I won't be forgetting this. You're a grand lady, and 'tis an honor serving you."

"Thank you, Jackson; you may go now," Belle said, touched by his declaration. She wasn't so wealthy that she didn't remember how it felt being dependent on another for the very bread in one's mouth, and she'd vowed never to make her employees feel as less than dirt beneath her feet. The way she'd been made to feel, she brooded, her expression troubled as she watched Jackson shuffle out of her study.

Three

One week later, Belle was in her rooms dressing for dinner at Lord and Lady Williton's, a prospect she viewed with glum resignation. The marquess and his simpering wife were friends of Georgiana's, and dull to the point of vapidity. She usually avoided their company whenever possible, but as tonight's party was in Julia's honor, she didn't see how she could gracefully decline. Duty, as she had learned at an early age, was seldom a pleasant thing.

She was adding the finishing touches to her toilet when there was a knock at the door and Julia drifted in, enchantingly attired in a gown of white and gold spangled silk.

"Good evening, Cousin!" she said, depositing a loving kiss on Belle's cheek. "How was your afternoon?"

"Uneventful," Belle answered, thinking of the round of calls she had made that day. "And yours? I trust you and Georgiana enjoyed your visit to the museum?"

A soft smile touched Julia's enticing lips. "Oh, yes." She sighed, her blue eyes sparkling. "It was wonderful."

"I see." Belle gave her a sharp look before turning to her abigail. "Thank you, Annette," she said, giving the young woman an encouraging smile. "You may go now."

The maid blushed and dropped an awkward curtsy. "Yes, Miss Portham," she said, her eyes downcast as she scurried from the room. Julia watched her go, a thoughtful look on her face.

"I think it is very kind of you to give the girl a position," she said, turning back to Belle with a smile. "Not many ladies would employ a servant who is lame."

"Annette cannot help her infirmity, and she gives me very good service," Belle responded, grateful the girl's mind was on something other than Tobias Flanders. In the week since they'd encountered him and Colford, it seemed Julia thought of little else.

"Yes, but to let her serve as your abigail, that is taking charity rather above and beyond, I think."

"Above and beyond what?"

"Noblesse oblige," Julia answered, casting Belle a considering look. "Tobias was telling me it is what is expected of members of our Society."

Belle was silent for a long moment, not certain which shocked her more—that Julia was on such intimate terms with Mr. Flanders as to refer to him by his Christian name, or that the dull-witted dandy was capable of such thoughts. She gazed into the mirror, pretending interest in her reflection as she sought to recover herself. When she felt more in control, she picked up the gold satin fan from the top of her dresser.

"A rather intriguing line of thought for a poet," she said, her eyes on the fan as she opened and closed it. "Might I ask when this conversation took place?"

Julia glanced away. "This afternoon," she confessed, lowering her eyes to her clasped hands.

"We met him at the museum ... quite by chance, of course."

"Of course," Belle returned absentmindedly, wondering how many other times the two had "accidentally" encountered each other in the past week. She and Julia were together most evenings, but the younger woman's days were usually spent either with Georgiana or one of her newfound friends, and until now, Belle had been pleased with the arrangement. If Julia was secretly meeting with that oaf Flanders, however, it was obvious changes would have to be made.

"Speaking of museums, I was wondering if Georgiana and I could attend the Royal Porcelain Exhibit," Julia said with a feigned interest that didn't fool Belle for a moment. "There was the most interesting article in *The Times* this morning, and I thought the exhibit sounded fascinating."

"Yes, I saw the article," Belle replied, remembering the effusive praise heaped on the display, one of Prinny's few acquisitions that had met with any approval. She'd thought at the time a visit to the exhibit sounded like a pleasant way to spend an afternoon.

"Why don't we all go?" she suggested, deciding it might be wise to keep a sharper eye on her ward in the future. "We can make a day of it."

As she expected, Julia leapt to her feet, her blue eyes wide with panic. "But that would ruin ... That is, I know how very busy you are, and I don't wish to be a bother."

The first niggling of suspicion was now a full-blown certainty, and she fixed the younger woman with a commanding look.

"You won't be a bother, my dear," she said, picking up her fan and rising to her feet. "In fact, the more I think of it, the more I think it will be just the thing. Shall we say next week?"

Julia opened her lips as if to protest, but after a moment she closed them with a sigh. "Next week will be fine, Cousin," she said, with a marked lack of enthusiasm.

After Julia returned to her own rooms, Belle went in search of Georgiana. She found her in the library, and when she mentioned her suspicions, her cousin confirmed them with a laugh.

"Well, of course she has been meeting Flanders, you silly goose! You must know she is enamored of him."

"And you must know I cannot abide that posturing fool!" Belle protested, feeling betrayed by Georgiana's actions. "How can you allow her to throw herself at him like that? You, who are forever lecturing me about her reputation!"

"She's not 'throwing herself at him,' " Georgiana corrected, her lips thinning in displeasure. "They are conducting a very proper courtship under my watchful eye, and I assure you there is no way anyone could possibly object. As for you not liking the fellow, what has that to do with it? *She* likes him, and that is the only thing that matters."

"But, Georgiana, Flanders is a dolt with no prospects to recommend him," Belle continued, shuddering to think of Toby as a member of her family. "You can't wish to see Julia wasted on that . . . that fribble."

Georgiana sat back in her chair, her expression stern as she studied Belle. "Again, my feelings are of no moment," she said with uncompromising bluntness. "Julia truly loves the lad, and if the mooncalf looks he has been casting her way are any indication, it is a sentiment he more than returns. If he should ask permission to speak to Simon, I don't see that it is any business of yours."

The unexpectedly harsh words struck Belle as cruelly as any whip. It was as if once again she was the unwanted outsider, the orphan who must be accommodated in the name of family honor. The old pain cut deep, and her instinctive response was to retreat. Drawing herself to her full height, she fixed Georgiana with her coolest stare.

"Simon may well be Julia's guardian," she acknowledged in frosty tones, "but she is still my responsibility. I promised Simon I would allow no harm to befall her while she is in my care, and that is a promise I mean to keep, whether it is any of my business or nay. I trust I have made myself clear."

To the young lady listening in the hallway, she had made herself all too clear, and with tears streaming from her blue eyes, Julia turned and dashed up the stairs.

"Another glass of champagne, Lady Bingington?" Marcus asked, bending solicitously toward Charlotte. "It is rather close tonight."

"Indeed it is," Lady Bingington replied, her cheeks bright with color as she vigorously fanned herself. "I cannot think what his lordship is about, ordering the fires to be kept blazing when he has close to fifty people stuffed into his drawing room."

"Williton has never been known for his good sense," Marcus answered, signaling one of the circling footmen with a lift of his finger. Seconds later the liveried servant was standing before them, presenting a tray to Marcus.

"The poor soul looked as if he could use this more than I," Charlotte commented, sighing with relief as she took a sip of the icy wine. "One of the first things I did once I was out of mourning was to design a more comfortable livery for the servants. They were going about their duties swathed in velvet even in the hottest weather."

"Your ladyship is very kind," Marcus said, meaning every word. The more he was around Charlotte, the more he became convinced she was just the lady to be his countess. Tonight he would probe her feelings to see if she reciprocated his interest. Time was rapidly running out, and if she should refuse, he would have to turn his sights elsewhere.

"More like I am a selfish creature who likes her comforts." Charlotte turned his praise aside with a light laugh, her brown eyes sparkling as she gazed up at him. "Servants swooning from the heat are of little use to anyone."

"Pragmatic and kind," Marcus murmured, availing himself of her free hand and carrying it to his lips. "You are indeed a paragon among ladies. How can I resist?"

Her answering laugh and the discreet but firm way she freed her hand from his boded ill for his courtship. "Oh, I am sure that shouldn't be a problem for a scamp like yourself," Charlotte retorted, turning to gaze about the room with studied interest. "Oh, look, is that not Miss Portham and Miss Dolitan? My, isn't she lovely? That is a stunning gown."

Marcus bit back his disappointment and glanced obligingly to the door where the two ladies and Mrs. Larksdale were greeting their host and hostess. Miss Dolitan was dressed in a sparkling white gown as befitted a debutante, while Mrs. Larksdale was rigged out in varying shades of purple. It was The Icicle, resplendent in emerald silk, who caught and held his attention.

The gown was simply, even primly cut, but it clung to her slender form in a manner that made the breath catch in his throat. Her glorious golden hair was caught back in a stylish chignon with only a few curls escaping to caress the high curve of her cheek. Emeralds glistened about her throat and winked from her small ears, and a large, square-cut emerald adorned the hand she was holding out to the marquess.

"I wonder who her modiste is," Charlotte said, her eyes resting on the ladies. "One of my nieces is to make her bows next year, and that is precisely the sort of gown I should like to see her wear."

Marcus tore his eyes from Miss Portham long enough to cast Lady Bingington a puzzled frown. "You would allow your niece to wear green?" he asked, faintly surprised, for the duchess had always struck him as a pattern card of propriety. "I thought debs were obliged to wear white."

"And so they are, but as it is Miss Dolitan's gown I am referring to, I see no problem," Charlotte returned, tipping her dark head to one side as she slanted Marcus a teasing smile. "What made you think I meant Miss Portham?"

Marcus was horrified to feel his cheeks warming with embarrassment. "Young debs hold no interest for me," he muttered, glancing about him for some potential diversion. His eyes lit on Toby, who was forging a path toward Miss Dolitan, and he turned to Lady Bingington.

"If your ladyship will excuse me, I must have a word with Toby," he said, executing a swift bow. "There is something of import I need to discuss with him."

"Of course, my lord," Charlotte agreed, granting his release with an understanding smile. "I see an old friend I've not seen in some years, and believe I shall go over to say hello. Good evening."

Marcus bowed again and hurried over to where Toby had already engaged Miss Dolitan in conversation. Miss Portham was standing to one side, her beautiful face frozen with disapproval as she listened to Toby's enthusiastic greeting of her ward.

" '... should pluck the feathered wings of time,' " Toby concluded, his heart in his eyes as he gazed at Julia. "Do you like it? I wrote it this afternoon after we had parted."

"I think it most wonderful." Julia sighed, an answering light gleaming in her eyes. "Byron is nothing compared to you."

Toby was puffing up with pride when he spied Marcus bearing down upon them. "I say, sir, she liked it!" he said, beaming as his cousin joined them. "Told you she would."

"And I told you, sir, to be more discreet," Marcus snapped, aware of the interested eyes that were studying them. He'd given up trying to discourage Toby's interest in the pretty deb, but he had warned him not to spout any more of his abominable poetry at her. Since his conversation with Miss Portham, he'd taken pains to learn more of Miss Dolitan's formidable brother, and what he had learned alarmed him. Simon Dolitan was rumored to be a hard and driven man, and Marcus much doubted he would approve of a man publicly composing odes to his innocent sister.

"Inspiration knows no restraints," Toby returned with airy indifference, carrying Julia's hand to his lips. "She is the most difficult but desirable of mistresses."

"Toby!"

"Mr. Flanders!"

Marcus and Belle both gasped out their objections and then exchanged angry glares. Belle was the first to speak, her golden eyes disdainful as she met Colford's icy gaze. "I think, my lord, that you might wish to have a word with your heir," she said, her cold voice giving no hint to the hot anger burning inside her. "He appears in need of instruction as to the correct manner of addressing young ladies of quality."

Marcus stiffened at the cutting words. Even though he fully intended pinning Toby's ears back for his recklessness, he wasn't about to do so at her command. Instead he reached out and grasped her by the hand. "I think first, Miss Portham, I will have a word with you," he said, his fingers closing strongly about hers. "This way." And he dragged her out into the garden, ignoring her indignant struggles to free herself.

"How dare you!" she cried the moment they were outside. "I insist you release me at once!"

"Gladly." He dropped her hand, his face set with fury as he glared down at her. "I've no wish to contract frostbite."

Belle's lips tightened at the clever insult, but she was hanged if she would let him know it hurt. "If you are quite finished insulting me, my lord, perhaps you'd care to explain yourself. I was hoping to avoid scandal; now it appears we have made our own. Or was that your intent?"

"What the devil is that supposed to mean?" Marcus demanded, with an irritated scowl.

"Merely, sir, that making scandal is something at which your family seems particularly adept," Belle said, chafing her wrists. She had very fine skin, and she knew her wrists would bear the marks of his fingers for some days to come.

Marcus scowled down at her. "If you are referring to that wretched wager Toby instigated between himself and St. Ives last year . . ."

"I am."

"Ha! I *knew* you would blame me for that!" he exclaimed, looking surprisingly smug. "I told Alex as much, but he assured me you were too kind a lady to act so unfairly."

Belle bit her lip, realizing she had been about to

do just that. Such an accusation would have been monstrously unfair considering he'd been in the country at the time, and she was honest enough to admit she owed him an apology. She was also human enough to know she would die sooner than utter it. A compromise was clearly in order, and after a moment's hesitation, she tipped her head back to meet his eyes.

"As it happens, sir, I in no way hold you responsible for Mr. Flanders's role in that unfortunate incident," she said, proud of the control she was displaying. "However, there is still the scandal you and the viscount caused over a certain female. Julia is a well-brought-up young girl, and care must be taken to insure she doesn't associate with any undesirable parties."

The moment the words left her mouth, Belle knew she'd committed a serious error. In a flash Colford's eyes had gone from soft gray to the color of ice. His full mouth thinned into a dangerous line, and the look on his face was enough to make her step back a pace.

"Be grateful, madam, that you are a woman," he said, his voice soft with the force of his anger. "Were you a man, I would call you out for such temerity."

Belle's cheeks paled, not so much from fright as from the admission that she had hurt him, cruelly and unfairly. It took every ounce of courage she possessed, but she stood her ground. "I apologize, my lord," she said, her soft voice even. "It was very wrong of me to say such a thing, and I would ask that you forgive me."

Her sincere apology took him aback, and his anger faded as quickly as it had erupted. He was by nature even-tempered, and he disliked being at odds with anyone. Even, he acknowledged with a rueful sigh, with the self-possessed young beauty gazing up at him with solemn golden eyes. "Apology accepted, Miss Portham," he replied, inclining his head. "And may I also apologize for dragging you out here without so much as a by-your-leave? As you say, it has doubtlessly created a dreadful scandal."

"I have endured far worse," Belle responded, grateful the awkward moment had passed. She'd never truly felt in any danger from Colford, but she'd also never seen a man who was so coldly furious. It was evident the earl took his name and honor very seriously, and she admired him the more for it.

"Now that you have me out here," she said, her voice thawing by several degrees, "perhaps you'd care to tell me what was so important, it couldn't wait for a more private occasion."

"Oh, that." Marcus's temper stirred at the memory of how she'd scolded Toby. "I wanted to discuss Toby with you. Unless I am much mistaken, you don't care for his suit, and I should like to know why. Is it because he is my heir?"

Belle blushed at his acuity. "Nonsense," she denied gruffly, lowering her head to avoid his steady gaze. "I assure you that has nothing to do with it. It is just—"

"Miss Portham—"Marcus's hand captured her chin, gently raising her face—"I think we both have sufficient *ton* to keep the truth between us. A hostile truth, mayhap," he acknowledged, his thumb lightly brushing over the pouting softness of her lip, "but the truth nonetheless. I would not have you change that now."

Heat suffused Belle's cheeks at his softly spoken words, and she sent him a resentful look. "That is part of it," she admitted, hating that he made her feel so mean, "but a small part only." She then went on to tell him of the many meetings between

their mutual charges, and her fear that the two
would end up, if not compromised, then at the
very least the target of some unpleasant tattle.

"As it happens, I agree with you," Marcus said
when she was done, and then smiled at her incredulous expression. "Why so shocked, Miss
Portham? I have already told you I take my responsibilities toward Toby very seriously."

Belle remembered their conversation in the park.
"Then you agree with me that their . . . infatuation
must not be allowed to continue?"

"Perhaps," he conceded, "but not perhaps for
the same reasons as you might think." At her puzzled look, he reluctantly related what he'd learned
about Simon Dolitan, and as expected, she reacted
with cool indignation.

"You make Simon sound like an ogre," she complained, folding her arms over her chest. "He is a
trifle hard, I grant you, but he loves Julia. He
would never object to her marrying a man she
loves and one who truly loves her."

"But that is precisely my point," Marcus replied,
thinking this was the oddest conversation he'd
ever had . . . and with The Golden Icicle of all people. "Toby falls in and out of love with depressing
regularity. Although his feelings toward Miss
Dolitan have endured longer than his other infatu-
ations, when he grows bored with her, I fear
Dolitan will take it amiss and express his displeasure on my heir."

That silenced Belle as she imagined Simon's reaction to any man treating his beloved younger
sister in such a cavalier manner. "What do you
suggest we do?"

Marcus folded his arms across his chest and
gave her a cool look. "Nothing."

She blinked at his blunt reply. "But you just
said—"

"Miss Portham, are you a student of Shake-speare?"

"Of course I am," she replied impatiently, wondering what that had to do with Julia and Mr. Flanders.

"Only think for one moment, Miss Portham. *Romeo and Juliet.* Star-crossed lovers parted by an ancient family feud. If we attempt to separate them now, we'll only succeed in driving them closer together. They might," he added, "elope."

Belle gave a gasp and covered her lips. "You're right. That sounds precisely the sort of thing that would appeal to a young girl's romantic sensibilities."

"To say nothing of Toby's poetic tendencies," Marcus added, his lips lifting in a slight smile. "I daresay he might even be persuaded to write an ode on the subject."

Belle was unable to hold back an answering smile. "I daresay he would," she said, knowing he was only trying to distract her. "Will it rhyme, do you think?"

"Only if he can find a word to match 'border,' " he said, thinking it a great shame she didn't smile like that more often. The Golden Icicle was far less intimidating with her lips curved as if in anticipation of a kiss.

"Then you are suggesting we should just let true love run its course?" Belle asked, her brows puckering as she considered the matter. "You'll forgive me, my lord, but that hardly seems advisable. It will only delay the inevitable, and in the end accomplish nothing."

"On the contrary, it will accomplish a great deal. No, hear me out." He held up a hand when she would have protested. "You say they have been meeting, if not in secret, then at least without your permission. Is that correct?" At her nod, he contin-

ued. "Can't you see such actions only add spice to
their courtship? The forbidden fruit is always the
sweetest, and so long as they feel you are standing
between them, they will be that much more determined to be together. Whereas if you were to grant
them permission to court . . ." His voice trailed off
meaningfully.

"The fruit would soon lose its flavor," Belle concluded, laying a finger on her lip. "Yes, I can see
how it might work. But what if it doesn't? Julia
could still be hurt, in which case Simon would be
certain to dismember Mr. Flanders, and in the
meanwhile we would have wasted the better part
of the Season. Also, what of Julia's other suitors?
So long as Toby is dangling after her, she refuses
to consider anyone else."

"Julia's suitors, I shall leave to you, and to the
murderous Mr. Dolitan," Marcus said decisively,
aware they'd been out on the terrace longer than
was prudent. "Will you be attending the Merricks'
ball tomorrow night?"

Belle flushed at his question, remembering Lord
Berwick had asked the very same thing. "Yes, we
are," she admitted, wondering if, like his lordship,
Colford would also beg a dance. She was horrified
to discover she didn't find the notion as unpleasant as she once would have done.

"Excellent; so are we," Marcus said, unaware of
her brooding thoughts. "We shall meet there and
continue this conversation. In the meanwhile I
would urge you not to judge poor Toby so harshly.
I know he can grate on one's nerves, but he is not
without his charms. He is a Colford, after all."
And he sent her a good-natured grin that had her
smiling in return.

"Indeed he is, my lord," she returned with a soft
laugh. "How foolish of me to have forgotten."

"And cruel," Marcus continued teasing as he

guided her back to the crowded drawing room. "You must know there is nothing so wounding to a man's vanity as to be forgotten. We men can bear anything except being ignored."

"I shall keep that in mind for future reference," Belle said, enjoying the rare sense of ease between them. Since coming into her great fortune, she'd been the constant target of fortune hunters, and she'd learned to view all men with a chary eye. Not that she would have to worry about Colford playing her up sweet for her money, she thought ruefully. He'd made his true opinion of her obvious years ago, and their temporary truce aside, she much doubted that opinion had changed.

They had reached the open doors, and Belle was about to step inside when the earl laid a staying hand on her arm. She gave him a questioning look.

"You will consider what I have said?" Marcus asked, suddenly loath for their conversation to end. "You will allow Toby to pay Miss Dolitan court?"

"I will consider it," Belle agreed, recalling her earlier conversation with Julia. "In fact, I even have a suggestion."

"What?"

She told him of the exhibition she and Julia were planning to attend, and he agreed to meet them there. "Although I think it would be best if we arranged it for tomorrow," he said decisively. "The longer we leave them to their own devices, the greater the risk of scandal. Besides"—he gave her a sheepish grin—"I'd intended to be there anyway so that I could hear a lecture the curator is giving. It sounded quite interesting."

The notion of Colford listening to a dry lecture on Chinese porcelains surprised Belle, a reaction she hid behind a quick smile. "Very well, sir," she said pleasantly. "We shall meet you there. However," she added, holding up a warning finger, "be advised that I intend keeping a sharp eye on him. As you said, he *is* a Colford, and as I have learned, such creatures bear close watching. I shall study Mr. Flanders with greatest interest, sir, as I shall study you."

To her surprise, his silver-colored eyes lit with laughter, and he carried her hand to his lips for the briefest touch. "Oh, I am counting on that, Miss Portham," he drawled provocatively. "I am counting on it."

Four

Belle's campaign began the next morning as she and Julia lingered over their morning tea. She'd lain awake long into the night before coming to the conclusion that the earl was right. Keeping the young lovers apart would only draw them closer. If she hoped to dissuade Julia from Mr. Flanders, then she would have to throw them together at every opportunity. With that thought in mind, she sent the young girl an innocent smile.

"What are your plans for this afternoon, dearest?" she asked, raising her cup to her lips.

Julia gave a guilty start, her hand hitting her fork and sending it to the floor. While one of the footmen raced to recover it, she blushed a pretty shade of rose. "Plans?" she echoed, visibly striving for insouciance. "Er . . . nothing . . . That is, I'd thought to go shopping. I need some new ribbons and . . . and other things."

"Really?" The younger woman's transparency struck Belle as highly amusing. "As it happens, I am also in need of a few fripperies, so perhaps I shall join you. Unless you have some objection?" she added, delicately arching her eyebrow.

The look of horror on Julia's face confirmed Belle's suspicions that a rendezvous had been in the offing.

"Oh no!" Julia denied, wondering if there was time to send Toby word their meeting would have to be canceled. "You must know your company is always welcome, dearest Belle."

"Good." Belle took another sip of tea. "After we finish shopping, what do you say we pop in and have a look at the Royal Porcelains? I know we spoke of going next week, but Lord Colford mentioned the curator would be giving a lecture, and I thought it sounded a most instructive way to spend an afternoon."

As quickly as they had plummeted, Julia's spirits soared again. "Toby . . . That is, Lord Colford and Mr. Flanders will be there?"

"Yes, and you could have tipped me over with a feather when he told me," she grumbled, contriving to look disgruntled. "One seldom finds rakes languishing amongst the porcelains, but I gather he is only going to accommodate Mr. Flanders."

That did surprise Julia, and she gave Belle a confused look. "Odd he did not say anything to *me*," she complained, feeling somewhat out of charity with her beloved.

"From what his lordship said, I gather it was a rather sudden decision," Belle answered with an indifferent shrug. "Well, what do you say? Shall we go?"

Julia decided to forgive Toby for neglecting to inform her of his plans. He was a poet, she reminded herself primly, and one could not expect such ethereal beings to remember such mundane things as porcelains. "Very well, Cousin," she said, her blue eyes sparkling with anticipation. "A visit to the museum sounds just the thing. Will Georgiana be joining us?"

"Unless she has other plans," Belle said, thinking she'd have a discreet word with the older woman to let her know of her change of heart. It would be just like her to help the youngsters arrange an elopement, she decided, remembering the surprisingly firm way she had championed Mr. Flanders's suit.

The rest of the meal continued in peaceful silence, and Belle was about to rise when Julia said, "Belle, may I ask you a question?"

"Certainly, my dear; what is it?"

"Well"—Julia's slender fingers fiddled with the handle of her cup—"last night when the earl escorted you out onto the balcony, what did you talk about? You were gone ever so long."

Belle didn't know whether she was amused or insulted by the chiding note in Julia's voice. Georgiana had said much the same thing, hinting darkly that five minutes longer and she and Lord Colford would have been expected to post the banns. "When he dragged me off, you mean," she corrected, taking care to hide her smile. "As for what we discussed, he took me to task for presuming to scold that foolish heir of his. And much as it pains me to admit it, I fear he is right."

Julia's jaw dropped in astonishment. "He is?"

"Mmm," Belle said slowly, knowing she would have to proceed carefully if she hoped to convince Julia her volte-face was genuine. "I have been thinking, and although I cannot approve of Mr. Flanders's rather frivolous turn of mind, I have come to the conclusion he is really not so objectionable. He is somewhat immature, of course, but I daresay that is something which will change with time." She was quiet for a moment, as if considering the matter. "That poem he quoted was actually quite good. Did he really write it?"

"Oh yes!" Julia exclaimed, her pride in Toby obvious. "He is a wonderful poet! One of his poems is even being considered for publication!"

"Is it?" The announcement didn't come as a complete surprise to Belle, considering much of the drivel currently being printed as "romantic poetry." "How nice."

"There is no money, of course, or at least very little," Julia rushed on, too happy to be discreet. "But I do not think that need concern us. I have more than enough blunt."

Only by calling on her years of control was Belle able to hide her shock. "You and Mr. Flanders have discussed this?" she asked, wondering if she was already too late.

"Only vaguely," Julia admitted artlessly. "The matter is much on his mind because of Colford's difficulties, but I assured him I didn't care for such things."

"Colford is having financial difficulties?" Belle asked, seizing on the one item of interest to her.

"Oh dear." Julia winced in chagrin. "I shouldn't have said anything. Toby swore me to secrecy."

"You needn't think I will say anything," Belle assured her, startled by her reaction to the revelation. Last year . . . last *week*, and the news that Colford was in the suds would have her rubbing her hands in glee. Now she was aware of an unsettling emotion that was more than concern and less than pity.

The assurance was all it took to loosen Julia's tongue as she revealed everything Toby had told her. "Well, it was none of Colford's doing, poor man," she said, leaning forward in a confiding manner. "His wastrel father squandered what blunt there was on the gaming tables and his ladybirds, and by the time his lordship came into the title, there was nothing left to inherit. Toby says he has been selling off his smaller properties for the last year or so, but it still isn't enough. That is why he is making a marriage of convenience."

"Toby?"

"Colford, silly! He has set his cap at the duke of Bingington's widow, and Toby says they are certain to marry by Season's end. He says he is praying it is so, otherwise he will be forced to throw himself on the matrimonial altar."

Belle was too stunned to speak. She remembered her conversation with Miriam at Almack's, and her heart sank to think of her proud adversary lowered to such a point. "Are things truly so bleak?" she asked, studying Julia through worried eyes.

"Worse," Julia continued eagerly. "Toby told me—in all confidence, mind—that Colford has had to sell off his stables, and that it is only by practicing the strictest economies they are to keep out of Dun territory."

"I see," Belle said quietly, her mind going to her own fortune. If she thought he'd accept, she would offer to lend him the necessary sums, but she knew such an offer would mortally offend him. Still, there had to be something she could do, she thought, turning her agile mind to the problem.

Seeing her cousin's dark expression, Julia gave a sudden cry. "Oh, no, Cousin!" she exclaimed, grasping Belle's hand. "It is nothing like that, I assure you!"

"Nothing like what?" Belle responded, wondering if she could buy up the earl's vowels and then arrange an equitable manner of payment. It could be done, and if she was very discreet, it was doubtful he would ever know.

"Toby holds me in the highest regard. He would never marry me for financial gain!"

Belle blinked in confusion. "I never thought he would," she said, and was unsettled to find it was so. Considering what she had just learned, the possibility should have been uppermost in her mind.

"I would never be so foolish as to allow myself to be used by a fortune hunter," Julia confessed with surprising heat. "Simon has been warning me against such creatures since I began putting up my hair, and if I even suspected Toby of harboring such aspirations, I should cut him dead in a heartbeat. But he is nothing like that, Belle, nothing."

Gazing into those earnest blue eyes, Belle felt her heart melt with sympathy. "I am sure he is not, my dear," she said, praying it was so. "But . . ."

"But what?"

Belle hesitated, hating to cause her ward the smallest pain, but knowing it was also her duty to prepare her for the cruel realities of a greedy world that measured so much by the contents of one's pockets. "But I feel it is something you must consider," she said at last, her tone gentle. "You are a wealthy young woman, and care must be taken to protect you from those who would seek to use you. I would be remiss in my duties if I were to fail to warn you, and that is what I am doing."

Julia's eyes filled with tears and she pushed herself back from the table. "You are wrong," she whispered, rising shakily to her feet. "Toby cares for me, not my money, and if it is the last thing I do, I shall prove it to you!"

"Julia, I didn't mean—" Belle broke off as Julia fled from the room with a sob. She watched her go with a feeling of dismay. Now she knew how Lady Capulet felt, she decided, reaching up to rub her throbbing temples. She'd always regarded the haughty woman as the villainess of the piece, but now she felt a certain kinship with her. Children, she decided with a heavy sigh, were the very devil.

* * *

Belle spent the afternoon going over account ledgers. Unlike most ladies of the *ton*, she believed in keeping a sharp eye on her money, not wishing to leave her independence to the honesty of others. And if truth were told, she enjoyed the challenge of deciphering her solicitors' scratchy handwriting.

She was adding a column of figures detailing her charitable contributions when she suddenly sensed she was no longer alone. She glanced up, her eyes widening at the sight of the slender brunette standing in the doorway, regarding her with mischief-filled green eyes.

"So this is how you conduct yourself when I am not here to keep an eye on you," the woman said, advancing toward her with a smile. "I might have known."

"Phillipa!" Belle exclaimed, tossing her quill down as she rushed around the desk to meet her friend. "When did you get back into town?"

"This morning," Phillipa, the viscountess St. Ives, said, returning Belle's embrace with a laugh. "Alex went rushing off on some mysterious errand, and so I thought I'd come over to see you. You look wonderful."

"So do you," Belle replied, holding her friend's hands as she stepped back to study her. "Wedded life would seem to agree with you."

Pip raised her eyes heavenward. "Not you, too," she grumbled as Belle led her to the settee set before the fireplace. "My aunt came to spend the holidays with us, and she had the nerve to say I *glowed*. Alex looked so pleased with himself, I was tempted to box his ears. Can you imagine?"

Belle laughed at her friend's disgruntled expression. Lord, it was good to have Pip back, she thought, her spirits soaring with pleasure. "Indeed

I can," she teased, ringing for tea. "Looking at you, I am reminded that only last year you were quoting your favorite axiom at me. 'Better the shroud than—' "

" 'The veil,' " Pip concluded, wrinkling her nose. "I know. But I still say I had the right of it. Not every man is as remarkable as Alex."

"So I have heard."

"Smugness ill becomes you, Arabelle," Pip said, her tone haughty. "Now, tell me how the Season is progressing. How is Julia doing? Surrounded by a dozen beaus, I daresay."

The maid appeared with the tea cart, and Belle waited until she'd closed the door behind her before answering. "Actually, Julia has several beaus, but there seems to be only one whose regard she returns." She paused for effect. "Tobias Flanders."

Pip promptly choked on her sip of tea. "*Toby Flanders?*" she gasped, staring at Belle in disbelief. "You cannot be serious!"

"Unfortunately I am." Belle sighed, staring down into the amber depths of her tea. "She adores the silly creature, and he seems to be equally infatuated."

"Well, what do you intend doing about it?" Pip demanded, setting her cup aside with a scowl. "I can't imagine your wishing to have him as a member of your family!"

"Heaven forbid," Belle said, "but for the moment Colford and I have decided it may be wisest to do nothing."

"Colford?"

Belle was hard-pressed not to laugh at Pip's expression. "You needn't look so horrified," she drawled, her golden-brown eyes sparkling with amusement. "His lordship and I were able to come to an agreement without killing each other. Although I must admit 'twas a near thing," she added, remembering her fury at the high-handed way he had dragged her off last evening.

"I can imagine," Pip said, studying Belle with interest. "Tell me everything."

Belle obliged her, describing Julia's regard for Toby and his apparent passion for her. She concluded by explaining the plot she and the earl had hatched, and was surprised when Pip gave an approving nod.

" 'Familiarity breeds contempt,' " she quoted, looking thoughtful. "How like a rake to think of something like that."

Belle picked up her cup of tea, confused by her urge to correct Pip. "I am taking Julia to the Royal Exhibition today," she said instead, her eyes not meeting her friend's. "Colford will be there with Toby, and we'll arrange it so he and Julia can meet. An exhibition sounds like a rather respectable place to conduct a courtship, don't you agree?"

"If you say so." Pip made a face. "Personally I cannot see anything respectable about those garish pots of Prinny's. He gave us one as a wedding present, and Alex is having a cabinet built for it."

Only Pip would sniff at a priceless Ming vase, Belle thought, shaking her head in mock despair. "How many times must I tell you you need to develop other interests?" she teased. "One cannot live and breathe politics alone, you know."

"I don't see why not. Alex and I do," Pip responded tartly, then gave a sudden grin. "Well," she admitted, her green eyes shining with a woman's knowledge, "perhaps we allow a *few* other things to take precedence."

Belle blushed at the daring remark, but she wisely refrained from comment. She and Pip began discussing their favorite subject and were arguing whether Castlereagh's new peace proposal for Italy would work when the butler announced an unexpected visitor.

"The earl of Colford, Miss Portham," he intoned with a bow. "He is in the drawing room asking if he might speak with you."

"The earl, hm?" Pip shot Belle a speculative look. "I knew you had made your peace with him, but I had no idea you were allowing him to run tame."

Belle blushed furiously, aware Gibson was listening to the exchange with well-bred interest. "He doesn't run tame," she muttered. "This is the first time he has been here since last year when he and St. Ives came looking for you."

"If you say so." Pip's eyes danced with merriment. She never thought to see the day her friend and the earl would end their hostilities, and she couldn't wait to share the news with Alex. "Well, why are you standing there, Gibson?" she demanded of the butler with a roguish grin. "Go and fetch the earl. It doesn't do to keep a peer of the realm cooling his heels, you know."

"As you say, my lady." Gibson bowed ponderously. "I shall . . . er . . . fetch his lordship at once."

After he had withdrawn, Pip turned to Belle. "I adore Gibson. Would you be angry if I were to steal him from you?"

"Furious," Belle replied, wondering if there was enough time to dash up to her rooms and change her gown. She didn't mind Pip seeing her in her rather worn gown of blue and rose merino, but it did pique her vanity that she should appear in front of his lordship looking less than her best.

She was about to excuse herself when Pip said, "That reminds me, Belle, where is your companion? In all the years I've known you, this is the first time I can recall seeing you without one of your ladies."

Belle thought of the succession of young women she had employed as her companion since coming to London. Her intention had been more to provide them with training and to avoid the scandal of living alone than out of a need for companionship. "Since I have Julia and Georgiana living with me, I've decided a companion would be superfluous," she said, crossing the room to stand in front of the mirror hanging above the mantelpiece. She could feel her chignon slipping and was attempting repairs just as the door opened.

"Miss Portham, Lady St. Ives." Marcus included both ladies in his graceful bow. "How delightful to see you again."

"My lord." Belle managed a polite smile. She could see Pip's expression as she glanced from Colford to her, and she longed to give her friend a pinch.

"I saw St. Ives as I was leaving Whitehall," Marcus said, addressing his remark to the viscountess. "He said I would probably find you here."

"Did he?" Pip tilted her chin at a defiant angle. "And pray how did he know where I might be? The wretch went tearing out of the house while I was still being presented to the staff. For all he may know, I could be sitting patiently at home awaiting his return like a dutiful wife."

A slashing dimple appeared in Marcus's lean cheek. "Somehow, Lady St. Ives, I much doubt such a thing even crossed Alex's mind," he drawled, amused at the notion of the little hellcat behaving with anything approaching propriety. "His exact words, and I am quoting, were 'When you see Miss Portham, pray tell my wife that I will be home for tea.'"

"Hmph." Pip pretended to be offended, an effect that was spoiled by the love glowing in her jewel-colored eyes. "By that I suppose he expects me to be there waiting for him. He is such an inconsiderate beast, Belle, you would not credit it."

"I am sure I would not," Belle answered, her eyes meeting the earl's over Pip's head. He was smiling, and for a moment a look of shared amusement flashed between them.

Pip gave a loud sniff, still piqued with her handsome husband. "You say you saw Alex at Whitehall," she said, turning an accusing look on the earl. "I take it then that he was gone there to discuss the Trade Acts? The devil, and after he promised to wait until after the debating session."

"Actually, I believe he only wished to call upon Lord Whitton," Marcus soothed, still amused. "His Grace had several items he wished to discuss with your husband."

"Pompous, deceitful Tory," Pip grumbled, not making it clear whom she was referring to. "So he thinks to have everything neatly sewn up before the debates even begin, does he? Well, we shall just see about that! Belle?" She glanced at her friend for support and was not disappointed.

"A tea?" Belle suggested, feeling a stir of interest. She had once sought to become a political hostess, and she was anxious to lend Pip any help that she could.

"Perhaps." Pip tapped a finger against her lip as she considered the matter. "Although a dinner party might be better. Politicians are much easier to charm once their bellies have been filled, don't you agree, my lord?"

"Much easier," Marcus replied, amused by her rather belligerent attitude. He'd thought Alex quite mad when he'd wed the fiery little bluestocking amidst a storm of gossip, but now he was beginning to think Alex had done precisely the right thing. There was something to be said for marrying a woman who shared your interests, he thought, his eyes resting on Miss Portham's classic features. He wondered if she would be as supportive as her outspoken friend.

"It would take some doing," Pip was saying, ignoring the earl's silence, "but with help, I think I shall be able to think of something. Belle, may I count upon your assistance?"

Belle swallowed uncomfortably. She truly wished to help, but she did not see how she could find the time. Her school and other charities took up a great many of her hours, and then there was the ball she was planning to officially launch Julia into Society. That would take place in less than a month, and there was still a great deal left to be done. On the other hand . . .

"Of course I shall be delighted to help you, Pip," she said, with a forced smile. "What is it you would like me to do?"

While the three adults were discussing the dinner part, Toby and Julia were meeting secretly in the library. "Had a devil of a time getting here without being discovered," he told Julia as he pressed a kiss to the back of her hand. "Colford almost saw me a dozen times. Now, what is this nonsense about your cousin trying to part us, eh?"

"Oh, Toby, it is all my fault!" Julia cried, raising tear-drenched eyes to his face. "I told her your cousin was sailing in deep waters, and now she thinks you mean to marry me for my money!"

"Devil you say!" Toby bristled with indignation. "No such thing; I'm a poet, not a blasted fortune hunter."

"I know that, but she doesn't," Julia said, raising a handkerchief to dab at her eyes. "It's not her fault, of course, for you wouldn't believe the way she has been courted for her fortune. The stories I

could tell you. . . ! Why, Simon told us our own
uncle attempted to seduce her in order to get his
hands on her fortune, and she was scarce sixteen
at the time."

"The blackguard!" Toby exclaimed, properly
shocked. "No wonder she's such a cold fish."

Julia gave a miserable nod. "Yes, and that is
what makes it so difficult to be angry with her.
She is only doing what she thinks right to protect
me."

"Rather like a guardian dragon, what?" Toby
chuckled and tilted his head to one side. "A
dragon," he said slowly, "like in an epic poem.
The lovely maiden locked in her tower and
guarded by a fierce dragon . . ." His voice trailed
off and he began composing stanzas in his head.

"Toby!" Julia recognized the faraway gleam in
his eye and gave his arm an impatient shake.
"What are we going to do?"

"Do?" He blinked down at her. "About what?"

"My cousin!"

"Don't think there's much we can do, my love,"
he said, eager to be gone so that he could write
while the poem was fresh in his mind. "Besides, I
don't see why you're enacting such a tragedy over
this. Miss Portham ain't your legal guardian, and
she can't forbid me to pay court to you. At least,
I don't think she can," he added thoughtfully,
wishing he'd paid more attention to such niceties.

"Are you certain?" Julia was gazing up at him
with worshipful eyes. "I couldn't bear to be parted
from you, even for a day."

Her words made Toby's chest swell with pride.
"Never think that, my love," he said, patting her
hand and feeling rather like the hero in one of
Byron's cantos. "Comes to it, I daresay I could
have m'cousin speak to your dragon. An earl,
even if his pockets are to let."

Julia considered that for a long moment. "It might work," she conceded, "although I am not so certain. Sometimes I have the impression she doesn't care for him overly much. I shall have to ask Lady St. Ives while she is leaving. If anyone would know—"

"St. Ives!" Toby blanched. "Lord, I didn't know that she-devil was here! I'd best take my leave before that jealous fiend she is married to decides to arrive. A madman, you know. He threatened to put a bullet through me on more than one occasion because of her."

"But, Toby . . ."

"Later, my dear." Toby pulled his beaver hat down about his eyes and began edging toward the door. "Not a word about my visit, eh? Wouldn't want that bluestocking to know I was here. There's a girl." He cracked open the door and, after a furtive glance about him, slipped from the room.

Five

The Merricks' home in Knightsbridge was alive with laughter and music when Belle and her cousins arrived. Julia was almost immediately surrounded by the group of young ladies she had met at previous balls, while several of Georgiana's friends arrived to carry her off. Only Belle was left standing in the doorway, and for a moment a feeling of almost overwhelming loneliness washed over her. She was about to go in search of the punch bowl when Lord Berwick walked up to greet her.

"Miss Portham," he murmured, his hazel eyes filled with admiration as he bent over her hand. "May I say how lovely you look this evening?"

"Thank you, my lord," she replied, pleased by his flattery. The gown was of her own design, and she felt the gold and cream striped silk conveyed the image of cool and regal elegance she was trying to project.

"Did you ever learn what became of your coachman? I trust he hadn't met with an ancient," Lord Berwick said as he guided Belle toward the ballroom, where the lilting strains of a waltz could be heard.

"Nothing so serious, thank heavens," she said, pleased he had thought to ask. "Apparently some-

one cut the reins while he was away from the carriage, and it took some time to repair the damage.
He was most distressed."

"I can imagine," Berwick replied with a low
chuckle. "Most employers would have been furious to discover their coachman tippling while on
duty."

"A pint of ale hardly qualifies as a 'tipple,' sir,"
Belle said, defending Jackson with a slight frown.
"He is an exemplary driver, and I would trust him
with my life."

"Your loyalty to your staff does you proud, Miss
Portham," the marquess said, patting the gloved
hand that rested in the cradle of his arm, "but it
never does to coddle one's servants. I trust you
gave the man the sack?"

Belle stiffened at the condescending tones.
"Then you would trust wrong, my lord," she said
frostily, her lips tightening in displeasure. "As I
have said, Jackson is an exemplary driver, and I
see no reason to dismiss him for one mistake ...
especially one that was none of his doing."

"Now I've offended you," he murmured, pulling her to a halt and sending her a contrite smile.
"I'm sorry, ma'am. I assure you I didn't mean to
sound so insufferably high in the instep. May I
hope you will forgive me?"

Despite her displeasure at his presumptuous-
ness, Belle decided it would be uncivil to remain
hipped, especially in light of his wry apology.
"Very well," she said, tilting back her head to
study his face. "You are forgiven ... for now."

Her reply seemed to amuse him, and he was
smiling as they resumed walking. "I might have
known you would be as cautious as you are gra-
cious," he said wryly. "And I must say I admire
you for it. It is always wisest to hedge one's bets."

"I had no idea that is what I was doing," Belle

commented, her eyes seeking out Julia as they entered the ballroom. She saw her out on the dance floor where a new set was forming, and was pleased to see her dancing with someone other than Toby.

"Caution is the hallmark of prudence," the marquess replied, "and as a politician, prudence is something I admire very much. These are uncertain times, and I feel England must move forward with the greatest care if we are to realize our destiny as a nation. Do you not agree?"

Belle gazed up at him in astonishment, trying to remember the last time a man had asked her opinion on a political matter. Then she realized one never had. Most gentlemen of her acquaintance seemed to think women incapable of discussing anything more weighty than fashion or the latest *on-dit*.

"Care must be taken, certainly," she began, her pleasure stirring, "but it must not be confused with complacency. Our world is changing every day, and we must take care to change with it least we run the risk of being left in the dust."

"My sentiments exactly, Miss Portham. How I wish certain members of Parliament shared your vision and your intellect. They move with painful slowness when it comes to such matters, and the very threat of change is enough to send them into the vapors."

Belle felt herself glowing at his words of praise. For the first time in months she began to reconsider her plan to marry for political gain. Lord Berwick not only shared her interests, but he seemed willing to encourage them; a definite change from most men, she decided, and then was annoyed to find herself thinking of Colford. She much doubted *he* would have praised her vision and her intellect when it came to political matters.

As they danced, she and Berwick continued their fascinating discussion. When he asked for a second dance, she hesitated only a few more moments before agreeing, something she rarely did. He escorted her to where Georgiana was waiting, and he was scarcely out of earshot before the older lady began quizzing her.

"Well, well, well, you are a deep one, I must say," Georgiana drawled, fanning herself with languid movements. "I never thought you were interested in Berwick."

"I'm not interested in him, Cousin," Belle denied, mindful as always of her privacy. "He did me a kindness the other day, and I was but repaying him. You refine on nothing."

"Hmph, don't try to cozen me, young lady," the other woman grumbled, looking most insulted. "I know better."

"Indeed, and on what bodily part do you base this secret knowledge?" Belle asked sardonically, amused by her adamant attitude. "Your ankle, perhaps?"

"No, you little imp, I am basing it on these"—Georgiana indicated her eyes—"and on this." She tapped her temple. "I ain't so old I don't know what's what. 'Tis plain as a pikestaff the two of you are smelling of April and May, and I must say I am relieved to see it. I was beginning to fear you was falling into spinsterhood."

"I am well over five and twenty, Cousin Georgiana," Belle replied with an amused drawl. "There are those who would say I have not only fallen into spinsterhood, I have landed and settled in for the duration."

"With your fortune?" Georgiana gave a loud snort. "Don't be silly, gel. You'd be as eligible as the freshest-faced deb, was you *my* age!"

Her fortune again, Belle thought, her heart sinking. Why did it always come down to that?

"But you mustn't think I disapprove," Georgiana continued thoughtfully. "Berwick would make a most acceptable match for you. A marquess, and possessed of a respectable fortune. Not like some I could name," she added with a loud sniff.

"To whom are you referring, ma'am?" For the second time that night her thoughts drifted toward the earl of Colford. Since learning of his strained circumstances, she'd been trying to think of some way to be of assistance to him. In the depressing event Toby and Julia did make a match of it, they would be related ... distantly, and she didn't want it whispered that she allowed her relations to suffer while she lived in luxury. At least, that was the explanation she gave herself.

"Most of the men in this room are halfway up the River Tick, and them that ain't are in debt to the moneylenders," Georgiana said with her usual grim bluntness. "I say latch on to Berwick and cart him off to the parson before some other female beats you to it. If anyone was born to be a lady, it is you."

"Thank you, Cousin ... I think," Belle drawled, wondering if she'd just been praised or cleverly insulted. With Georgiana it was occasionally difficult to tell the difference.

The fact she'd stood up with Berwick hadn't gone unnoticed, and Belle spent the next hour declining offers from a variety of hopeful gentlemen. Finally she was forced to retreat to the terrace to escape the importunities of several rather persistent fortune hunters, and she'd no sooner reached her haven when she heard footsteps behind her.

"Miss Portham, I was wondering—"

"No, I do not wish to dance," she interrupted,

not turning around. "If you please, I'd rather be left alone."

There was a moment of silence, and then an amused voice drawled, "I am, of course, devastated by your refusal, but do you think you might let me ask before throwing the offer in my face?"

Belle whirled around as she recognized Lord Colford's husky tones. "My lord!" she exclaimed, grateful the moonlight hid her look of mortification. "Forgive my rudeness, but I thought you were one of those tiresome puppies who have been plaguing me."

"What tiresome puppies? Give me their names, and I shall call them to accounts at once," Marcus teased, enjoying the play of light and shadow across her face. He'd arrived less than ten minutes ago, and had wasted no time seeking her out. At the time he'd told himself it was because he wanted to settle this business with Toby, but gazing down at her, he wondered if that was all there was to it. He immediately pushed the uncomfortable thought to the back of his mind.

"They are of no importance," Belle said, dismissing them with an impatient wave of her hand. "Is Mr. Flanders with you?"

"Unfortunately," Marcus replied, grimacing at the memory of the battle he'd waged to get his heir to accompany him. After waiting impatiently for Toby to join him, he'd gone upstairs to discover him holed up in his study, scribbling what he called his "ode to a dragon." It had taken considerable effort on his part to pry him loose, but in the end he'd prevailed.

"Why do you say that?" Belle asked curiously, noticing the impatience that flashed across his face. "He's not bosky, is he?"

"Aye, but not on spirits," Marcus grumbled, and at her blank look added, "He was deep in the throes of creativity when I reminded him of the ball, and he was ill pleased when I insisted he accompany me. Ah well, I am sure Miss Dolitan will charm him out of the sulks. He was leading her out onto the dance floor the last I saw of him."

His words reminded Belle of her embarrassing faux pas, and she hurriedly sought to change the subject. "Speaking of Julia, what did you think of today's outing? It went rather well, don't you think?"

"By 'rather well,' I take it you are referring to the fact that Miss Dolitan scarce said more than three words to Toby the entire time we were there," Marcus said, recalling the stiff silence that had existed between the younger members of the party.

"He was hardly any more civil to her," Belle responded in Julia's defense. "But yes, that is precisely what I meant. Do you think it is working?"

"Possibly, although it is too early to abandon our plans just yet. Have you any other ideas in mind?"

"Well, I thought we might take them to see the Marbles and other public events," she said after a moment's consideration. "We'll take them for rides in the park and allow them the freedom accorded courting couples ... properly chaperoned, of course."

"Of course."

"And if worst comes to worst, you can bring Toby to tea every day until she cannot bear the sight of him," Belle concluded, ignoring the hint of laughter in his deep voice. "If that doesn't do the trick, then we'll think of something else. There, what do you think?" She gave him a triumphant look.

"It does have its merits," Marcus agreed at last, his tone thoughtful. "There are risks involved, but

I suppose that cannot be avoided in any endeavor."

"What risks?" Belle demanded, annoyed he should find fault with her plan.

"To begin, rather than parting our tiresome lovers, we might only succeed in drawing them closer together," he said bluntly, his gray eyes meeting hers. "An unlikely occurrence, I grant you, but it is a possibility we must consider. As is the possibility their affection is genuine. Have you thought about that?"

Belle's eyes wavered, but she managed to hold his gaze. "Of course I've thought about it," she said, feeling a sudden awkwardness. "And naturally if their feelings should prove to be lasting, I shall reconsider the situation."

"All right." He decided to let the matter pass for the moment. "What about the other risk we are running? The risk to ourselves? You must know that if we follow this plan of yours, we will become the targets of a great deal of eager speculation. People will assume *we* are the ones who are courting."

She hadn't considered that, she admitted silently, but now that she did, she could see that he was right. That is what people would think, and she supposed she couldn't blame them. A week ago such a suggestion would have had her screaming a furious denial; now she merely shrugged.

"I don't think that should prove an insurmountable problem," she said with considerable calm. "We have only to deny it, and in any event, we both have other escorts. Once we are seen with other people, that should put an end to the tattle." She thought of Lady Bingington and Julia's confidence that he would be making her an offer within a few weeks.

"That is so," he said, thinking of Berwick. "Then you don't mind having our names linked?"

"Certainly not," she denied huffily, turning away to gaze out over the small patch of green that passed as a garden. "When nothing comes of it, people will find some other excuse to wag their tongues. It will be forgotten in a fortnight."

"Perhaps," Marcus agreed, watching her speculatively. Despite his concern for Toby, he found he was equally concerned for her. Only last year he'd watched St. Ives suffer the pain of the damned as he'd struggled to spare his fiancée from the gossip caused by a foolish wager, and he had no intention of following suit. Miss Portham might be an annoying little vixen, but he wasn't about to have her reputation made fodder for the *ton*'s delection. At the first hint of talk, he would take steps to put an end to the tattle.

The ride in the park the following day went as smoothly as Belle could have liked, for unless she was much mistaken, Julia was decidedly cool to Mr. Flanders. He also seemed somewhat distant, although the cause for this might have lain with his preoccupation with his writing. Colford confided rather disgustedly that the younger man had spent most of the night scribbling away on his poem, driving him mad with his creative airs and his constant demand for words that rhymed with dragon.

The next day's ride through the park was equally strained, and as she watched the young couple riding ahead of them in sullen silence, Belle turned to the earl.

"The course of true love appears to be rather stormy this morning," she said, with a slight smile. "Am I to take it Mr. Flanders is still in the grips of his muse?"

"In the grips of something, at any rate," Marcus replied darkly, shooting Toby a speaking glare. "He was up again half the night, wandering about the house in his shirt sleeves and talking to himself. Jameson, my butler, took me aside this morning and tactfully suggested that I have him bled."

"Will you?"

"I would if I thought it would do a whit of good." Marcus shifted in his saddle and a grinned. "And what of Miss Dolitan? Shall I send the leech to your house once he has finished with Toby?"

"I think leeches are unnecessary at this time, my lord," she said after a moment's consideration. "Julia has been down in the sulks of late, but Georgiana assures me 'tis nothing to fret over. She says young girls are prone to these moods and that I mustn't pay them any mind."

"Sage advice," Marcus agreed. "But then, you must remember what it was like when you were that age. 'Ah, youth, what a shame to waste it on the young,'" he quoted, shaking his head with a mournful sigh.

Belle managed a slight smile. In truth, she hadn't a notion what it was like to be nineteen ... a normal nineteen, she amended unhappily. At that age she'd been embroiled in a bitter wrangle to wrest control of her fortune from her grasping relations, and the fight had left her even more withdrawn and distrustful of people. It was only in the last year or so that she had been able to lower her guard with others, and she wondered wistfully if she would ever be as open and carefree as her ward.

Marcus was also lost in bittersweet memories of his nineteenth year. Even at that tender age he'd known the responsibility for saving Colford would fall to him, and he'd watched with impotent fury as his father ran through the remaining inheritance. Part of him had longed to say the devil with it all and run away, to the sea perhaps, or even to America, where he could make a new life for himself. But the demands of duty and blood had prevailed, and here he was at five and thirty in debt up to his eyebrows and facing the grim realization that despite all he had done, it was still not enough. If he didn't make an advantageous marriage soon, all would be lost.

As they fell into a troubled silence, Toby finally emerged from his creative fog to notice the icy fury emanating from his companion. Studying her sulky expression, he cleared his throat and said, "I say, Julia, you ain't sickening after something, are you? You've been acting dashed odd these past few days."

Julia's head shot up. "*I've* been acting odd!" she exclaimed, her blue eyes flashing with indignation. "And what of *your* behavior? You've scarce said three words to me all morning, and that was about that silly poem you have been writing."

Toby stiffened at the cutting words. "I beg your pardon, Miss Dolitan," he said in perfect imitation of his formidable cousin. "I had no idea you found my writing so tiresome. My apologies if I was boring you."

"Well, you were," Julia snapped peevishly, feeling perilously close to tears. "It is all you talk about these days ... when you talk at all."

For someone who'd spent most of his life being berated for his loquaciousness, Toby had no idea how to respond to such a charge. He glared at her, wracking his brain for some proper response. "Oh, really?" he managed at last.

"Yes, really!" Julia retorted with another glare. "And then there was the cowardly way you crept from my cousins' house, like a naughty little boy hiding from his governess's wrath."

"Little boy!" Toby howled, his pride stinging at the belittling description.

"Naughty little boy," she corrected with a tearful toss of her head. "I'd never thought to see you behave in such an unheroic manner, Toby, and I quite wonder what I ever saw in you. Cousin Julia is right; you are nothing more than a ... a ... poetry-spouting dandy!"

Toby's round chin firmed with fury at what he considered the ultimate insult. He drew himself up to his full height and sent her a look fairly dripping with disdain. "And you, Miss Dolitan, are naught but an empty-headed little goose," he accused, proud of the cold hauteur in his voice. "Now, if you will excuse me, I believe I shall return to my one and true love ... my muse." And with that he dug his heels into his horse's side, leaving a sobbing Julia behind in a cloud of choking dust.

"And he rode off? Just like that?" demanded Alexander St. Ives, the Viscount of St. Ives, his dark blue eyes twinkling with amusement as he studied the earl's stern expression. "I wish I might have been there to see it."

"No, you don't," Marcus answered, grimacing as he raised his snifter of golden brandy to his lips. "When the damned fool went galloping off without so much as a by-your-leave, he left me to deal with a crowd of gawking gossipmongers and one very hysterical chit. Can't say as I appreciated it."

"Only one?" St. Ives arched an eyebrow mockingly.

"Miss Portham remained composed," Marcus replied, smiling at the memory of the efficient way she'd bustled Julia home. "In fact, had it not been for her cool presence of mind, the whole thing would have certainly ended in scandal."

A sardonic smile spread across St. Ives's tanned features. "Of course," he drawled mockingly. "How foolish of me to think The Golden Icicle would thaw enough to show genuine emotion."

The laughter died in Marcus's eyes at the derisive comment. Although he'd been the one to first call her that, he found he was suddenly loath to hear anyone, even an old friend like Alex, refer to her with such a marked lack of respect. Setting his glass down, he fixed Alex with a hard look.

"I will thank you, my lord, not to speak of Miss Portham in that manner," he said coldly. "She is a very kind lady, and I will not have her disparaged."

Alex's eyes widened at the note of deadly warning in Marcus's husky voice. "I meant no disrespect, I assure you," he said, taking care to hide his surprise at Colford's championing of the icy blonde. "Miss Portham is one of my wife's dearest friends, and I would never think of saying anything to her detriment."

Marcus relaxed slightly, realizing he had overreacted to the viscount's teasing words. "I am aware of that," he said, picking up his glass and staring at the amber liquid. "I didn't mean to snap at you like that. I suppose it is just because I am feeling a trifle guilty."

"Guilty?" Alex was intrigued. Last night Pip had mentioned she thought something was brewing between the two, but he'd dismissed the suggestion with an amused laugh. Now he wasn't so certain, and he had to admit 'twas an intriguing possibility.

Marcus traced the gilded rim of his snifter with the tip of his finger. "I'm the one who fastened that name to her, and merely because she rejected my advances . . . as rightly she should have done. I doubt she will ever forgive me." And he took a deep swallow of the fiery liquor.

Alex watched him in silence, wondering how much he could reveal of Miss Portham's past without violating his wife's confidence. "Phillipa assures me Miss Portham's true nature is as warm and generous as her own," he began, deciding it was as close to the truth as he dared get for the moment. "And given that, I think we may safely assume she has already forgiven that young man for his indiscreet actions and even more indiscreet words."

"Perhaps." Marcus winced as he remembered the remark he'd made about frostbite a few nights earlier. "Not that I suppose it matters. Now that Toby is no longer mooning after Miss Dolitan, there is no reason to assume we will be seeing so much of each other."

"I wouldn't be so sure of that," Alex said, thinking of Pip's plans for a ball. "In the meanwhile, are you certain it is truly ended between the two of them? Young lovers often quarrel and part. 'Tis considered de rigueur, or so I am told."

That brought Marcus's brows together in a frown. "Fairly certain," he said, recalling the vehemence in Toby's voice as he denounced his former ladylove. "He called her a silly chit, and vowed to have no more to do with her."

"That is no true indication of a man's feelings," Alex replied with a laugh, folding his arms across his chest and leaning back in his chair. "I recall saying the same thing about Phillipa, and look at me now."

"An appalling sight, I agree.' Marcus smiled at the happiness evident on his friend's face. "But in this case I think we can rule out a similar happy ending. The last I saw of Toby, he was holed up in his room and muttering something about Saint George."

"The dragon slayer?" Alex looked puzzled.

Marcus nodded. "He seems obsessed with the creature of late," he said with a low chuckle, "and I have decided I am better off not knowing why."

"Perhaps he has decided to become a knight?" Alex suggested, his dark blue eyes gleaming with laughter.

"Perhaps, and so long as he doesn't take to jousting with the servants, I've no objections." Marcus dismissed the matter with an indifferent shrug. "Now, enough of Toby; I have something else I need to discuss with you. Have you thought of what you are going to say at the debates?"

"Of course."

"Well?" Marcus demanded when he didn't elaborate.

Alex gave him a lazy smile. "Do you honestly think I mean to tell you my plans so that you can prepare a counter-strategy?" he drawled with evident amusement. "You forget I spent half my life in the military, and if I learned nothing else in all those years, it was not to reveal my intentions to the enemy. You shall hear my thoughts on the Trade Act on Thursday, my lord, and not a moment before. By the by, what are *you* going to say?"

Marcus leaned back in his chair and gave Alex a challenging look. "Go to the devil, my lord," he said, most cordially.

Three days later, Belle was in her rooms preparing for her visit to the school when Georgiana came stalking in, her lips pursed in annoyance.

"You must do something, Belle," she announced as she took her seat. "I refuse to endure this torture another moment!"

Belle gave a weary sigh, her eyes closing as she pinched the bridge of her nose. The last few days had been sheer hell for everyone, and the last thing she needed was one of Georgiana's scenes. She cast about in her mind for whatever might have overset her cousin, and decided she must be complaining about Julia's recent antics.

"I am sorry if Julia's behavior is distressing you, Cousin," she said icily, seizing upon the first explanation that came to mind. "But as you yourself told me, she is only sulking. It will pass."

Georgiana's expression grew even more sour. "Goose!" she accused impatiently. "You must know I'm not talking about Julia! I am talking about my ankle."

"Your ankle?"

"It has been throbbing all afternoon," Georgiana said, seeming surprisingly pleased about the matter. "Sharp pains like needle jabs, and deep, dull aches like the ague. It's never done that before, and I can only assume some dreadful tragedy is about to befall us all. *That* is what you must do something about."

Belle opened her mouth to administer a sharp setdown, and then closed it with a dispirited sigh. It would do no good, and in any case, she recalled hearing that it was sometimes best to humor the mad. "What would you suggest I do?" she asked, striving for a calm she was far from feeling.

"How am I to know?" Georgiana responded with a scowl. "I predict calamities; the very least you might do is prevent them."

"Very well, Georgiana, I shall do my best," Belle replied quietly, the headache that had been plaguing her off and on all day returning with a vengeance. She knew from experience that if she didn't rest, it would blossom into a full-blown migraine by day's end. Unfortunately Mrs. Langston and the children were expecting her, and she wasn't about to disappoint them because of a mere headache.

"See that you do." Georgiana's tone was less sharp now that she'd had her way. "We've already suffered one unhappiness this week, and I'd as lief not endure another."

"Yes, Georgiana."

The meek tones brought a frown to Georgiana's face. Had it been anyone other than Belle, she would have accused her of sarcasm, but she doubted her self-contained cousin would ever stoop to such common behavior. Her eyes narrowed thoughtfully as she studied Belle's face, noticing for the first time the marks of pain in her strained features.

"I say, Belle, ain't feeling sick, are you? You look positively out of curl to me."

The rather apt phrase brought a slight smile to Belle's lips as she rose to her feet. "I'm fine," she assured Georgiana. "It is only that I have a slight headache."

"Ah." Georgiana gave a wise nod. "Mayhap you have inherited my ability," she said, not certain if she cared for the idea.

"Or mayhap it is the weather," Belle returned, trying not to shudder. "It has been uncommonly hot these past few weeks."

"Yes, that is so." Georgiana brightened, deciding inclement weather was better than the possibility of sharing her power. "Mind you lie down this afternoon so that you'll be rested for the viscountess's dinner party."

The thought of Pip's first official function as the Viscountess St. Ives was almost enough to chase away the steadily increasing pain. She'd already had the small tea, of course, but that hardly counted. "I'll rest when I return from visiting,"

Belle promised, tugging on her yellow gloves as she strode to the door. "What will you and Julia be doing?"

"Shopping," Georgiana responded with a grimace. "The little minx has evidently decided Bond Street is the perfect panacea for a broken heart. You'll have to have a word with her before she drives that cold-eyed brother of hers onto the rocks."

Considering how plump Simon's pockets were, Belle considered that an unlikely event. Nevertheless, she did promise to speak to Julia, and her expression was thoughtful as she made her way down the stairs. Julia's behavior had been rather odd of late, she mused, nodding absentmindedly to Gibson as he held the door for her. One moment she would be as happy and carefree as a child, and in the next she would be weepy and teary-eyed. It made no sense, and she wished she knew what to do.

The footman standing attentively was new to her, but as she recalled Gibson muttering something about taking on new staff, she dismissed the matter with a shrug. She glanced up at the carriage box, more from reflex than anything, and started to climb into the carriage. Her foot was on the first step when she suddenly froze, her eyes darting back to the hunched figure in the many-caped coat.

"You're not Jackson," she said, her eyebrows drawing together in a frown. "Who are you?"

The man's shoulders twitched, but he didn't turn around. "Cashton, miss," he said in a gravelly whisper. "Jackson's . . . er . . . sick."

"Sick?" Belle was torn between suspicion and concern. "Why wasn't I informed? Where is he? What is going on here?"

"I warned him this wouldn't be easy," the

coachman said, his voice sounding oddly familiar to her. "He never listens."

"Who never listens?" Belle began backing away from the carriage, her heart pounding with trepidation. The footman and another man she hadn't noticed before crowded behind her, sealing off her one avenue of escape.

"Get in the carriage, Miss Dolitan," the man dressed as a footman said, closing his hand around her elbow and urging her forward. "We mean you no harm."

Belle was too frightened to notice the man's mistake. Instead she began struggling, wriggling frantically in a desperate effort to gain her freedom. She managed to tear her arm free, and struck her assailant in the face with her fist. He released her with a curse, his gloved hand cupping his streaming nose. She opened her mouth to scream, but before she could utter a syllable, another hand was clapped roughly over her mouth and she was dragged backward.

Acting on impulse, she sank her teeth into the hand, holding on until she tasted blood. Once more she was free, but before she could do more than draw a shaky breath, there was a rush of air by her ear. She tried to avert her head, but it was too late, and the world exploded with bright light and pain, catapulting her into darkness as she slumped in her captor's arms.

Six

"Blast and hell!" Marcus exclaimed, throwing down his pen in disgust. "Is there no end to this wretched tangle?"

"Certainly, my lord." Johns, Marcus's secretary for the past three years, replied in his pedantic manner, pushing his wire-rimmed spectacles back on his peaked nose as he studied his own list of figures. "In fact, I estimate that if you manage to keep current with the interest, you should have the estate free of debt in less than five years."

Marcus clenched his jaw, holding back an oath that would doubtlessly have made Johns swoon with horror. "Unfortunately I don't have five years," he muttered, rubbing the back of his neck with a heavy sigh. He and his secretary had been laboring over the accounts since luncheon, and never had the situation seemed more bleak. He'd been steadily whittling away at the mountain of debt he'd inherited, and still there was no end in sight.

"There must be some arrangement we can make," Johns said tentatively, although, like his master, he thought it unlikely. "The tradesmen have been most reasonable, and I am sure, with a bit of persuasion, they could be made to come about. You are the earl of Colford, after all, and they ought to be grateful for your custom."

"Gratitude won't fill their children's empty bellies," Marcus returned bluntly, pushing aside his weariness and picking up his pen again. "And in any event, that isn't our main problem. The tradesmen I might be able to come to terms with, but those to whom my father owed gaming debts are beginning to push for their money. If I can't find a way to pay them, I may have no choice but to sell the estate."

Johns nervously cleared his throat. "I don't believe that is possible, your lordship," he began, shuffling his papers. "According to the laws of primogeniture—"

"You needn't quote the law to me, Johns!" Marcus snapped, his gray eyes icy with fury. "I am painfully aware of what I can and cannot do with an entailed estate. But I don't see that in the end it will make one whit of difference. If I don't sell Colford to settle the debts, it will be seized by the crown for payment of those debts. The end result will be the same, but at least if we do it my way, I shall have some sense of honor . . . whatever consolation that might be," he added with a bitter smile.

Johns seemed at a loss for words, knowing his grim-faced employer was right. "There is another alternative," he began after a troubled pause. "I have hesitated mentioning it until now, but if things are so desperate, perhaps you—"

"If you are referring to a marriage of convenience, I've already thought of it," Marcus interrupted impatiently, thinking of Lady Bingington. In between his duties at Parliament and dealing with Toby's creative nonsense, he'd continued courting Charlotte, with mixed results. He was fairly certain she guessed his intentions, but he had no idea how she felt about it. She hadn't gone out of her way to encourage him, but neither had she actively discouraged him. It was as if she hadn't yet made up her mind, and he wondered how long he could allow the situation to continue unresolved. In the event she did refuse his suit, he would need time to begin courting another widow, or even a rich Cit, if worst came to worst.

"Yes, I've heard whispers you have been courting Miss Portham, and I must say I applaud your good sense," Johns said with a satisfied nod. "Rich as can be, and a beauty in the bargain. You could do far worse for Colford, I can tell you."

"Miss Portham?" Marcus glowered at the smaller man. "I was referring to the duchess of Bingington."

"A lovely lady, but not so well heeled as Miss Portham," Johns said, waving his delicate hand in dismissal. "I think you must reconsider, my lord, and offer your title to Miss Portham instead. She is but a lesser member of the gentry, and I daresay she would be more than willing to pay for the privilege of being called Lady Colford."

For a moment the image of Belle as his countess tantalized Marcus, but he dismissed it with an angry scowl. He and The Golden Icicle may have overcome some of their antipathy, but he wasn't fool enough to think she would accept his suit. She'd been on the Marriage Mart for years, and had she meant to sell herself for a coronet, she could have done so long ago. Besides, he admitted reluctantly, he admired her too much to offer for her when he did not love her.

"I am not interested in Miss Portham," he said, sending his secretary a warning glare. "We will not discuss her again."

Johns recognized the cold look his employer was giving him and began gathering up his papers. "Very well, my lord," he said, his prim mouth held in a manner that conveyed his disapproval. "Will there by anything else?"

"Yes, I want you to send one of the footmen to the jeweler's with the last of the diamonds. They ought to fetch enough to placate my father's gaming cronies for the moment."

"The diamonds!" Johns paled in horror. "But, sir, they have been in your mother's family for over seven generations! How can you even consider selling them?"

Marcus's gray eyes iced over with pain. "Because I have no choice," he said tersely, banishing to the back of his mind the memory of his sweet mother dripping in the fabulous jewels. "Just see to it, damn it."

"Yes, my lord," Johns said with a discouraged sigh before slipping silently from the room.

After the door closed behind him, Marcus crossed the room to pour himself a generous splash of brandy. God, did the little worm think he enjoyed selling his inheritance? he brooded, his expression savage as he downed the fiery liquor in a single gulp. It was like selling off pieces of himself bit by painful bit, and the anguish of it was more than he could bear. Curse his wastrel of a father, he thought angrily, hoping the old reprobate even now was paying for the evil he had done in his life.

Marcus was pouring a second glass when the door to his study burst open and Toby rushed in, his usually ruddy face almost white with panic.

"It was an accident!" he exclaimed before Marcus could speak. "They was supposed to kidnap her, not hit her!"

Marcus stared at Toby in disbelief, wondering if he'd finally gone mad. "Who was supposed to kidnap her?" he asked carefully, recalling that it was sometimes wisest to humor the insane.

"Gilford and Shipfield," Toby answered, his brown eyes earnestly beseeching Marcus. "Told them to carry her off like in the poems. Dashed good plan when you think of it; romantic and forceful, bound to work. But they grabbed the dragon instead, and now I don't know what to do."

"Your friends have kidnapped a dragon?" Marcus asked, wondering how great the scandal would be when Toby was carted off to Bedlam.

"They wasn't supposed to, mind," Toby stressed, grateful his cousin seemed to be taking the news so well. "They was supposed to take my beloved so that I could gallop to her rescue like a true hero, but they made a mistake. I . . . I think they may killed her," he concluded, his voice shaking with fear.

It was the fear in his voice that made Marcus realize that Toby was in earnest. He set the glass down carefully, recalling everything Toby had said. His beloved was evidently Miss Dolitan, unless he'd fallen in love with someone else in the past three days. And that must mean that the dragon . . .

"Oh, my God!' He whirled around to stare at Toby, his face paling with terror. "Are you talking about Miss Portham?"

"It was an accident," Toby repeated, close to tears. "They weren't supposed to hurt her, but she began struggling and Gilford panicked. He said he didn't hit her that hard, but she won't wake up and there's so much blood—"

Marcus leapt forward, grabbing Toby by the front of his jacket and giving him a vicious shake. "Where is she?" he demanded, his eyes blazing with fury. "What the hell have you done with her?"

"I . . . she is in the carriage, outside," Toby gasped, plucking ineffectually at the powerful hands holding him captive. "Thought about taking her home, but it didn't seem right, just leaving her on the sidewalk."

Marcus flung him impatiently aside and rushed outside, where he saw Miss Portham's carriage waiting at the curb. He tore open the door, his heart stopping when he saw a young man, his face pale with fear, cradling Miss Portham in his arms.

"She . . . she seems to be breathing, sir," the young man offered tremulously, holding a bloodstained handkerchief to her temples. "Perhaps it is just a fit of the vapors?"

Marcus ignored him, his concentration centered wholly on Miss Portham. Her eyes were closed, and her blond hair lay in a tangle about her alarmingly white cheeks. The breath barely moved from between her parted lips, and beneath the maroon velvet spencer he could detect the slight movement of her chest. Fighting back a cold wave of nausea that threatened to swamp him, he reached out to touch her cheek.

"How long has she been unconscious?" he demanded, hardly recognizing his own voice.

"Not long," replied the second man, dressed as footman, his eyes not quite meeting Marcus's. "Fifteen minutes, perhaps twenty. We came directly here once we'd realized our mistake."

"Have you sent for a doctor?" Marcus demanded, aware of a deep and deadly fury beneath his fear.

The two men exchanged nervous looks. "We—we were hoping it wouldn't prove necessary," said the man holding Miss Portham. "Bound to cause a scandal, and—"

"Go fetch Dr. Barker on Harley Street," Marcus interrupted, reaching into the carriage and plucking the unconscious woman from his arms. "Then I want you to go to Miss Portham's home and bring her cousins and her maid here."

"But, my lord—"

Marcus's gray eyes met his. "Do it."

The younger man quailed beneath the impact of that menacing silvery gaze. "Yes, my lord."

Cradling his burden against his chest, Marcus stepped back from the carriage, his expression cold as he gave the occupants a look of contempt. "Which of you is Gilford?" he asked, his voice soft with menace.

The man who'd been holding Miss Portham moistened his lips. "I—I am, Lord Colford," he said, his voice shaking with fear.

"Leave London," Marcus ordered. "If I ever see you again, I vow I shall kill you." And he turned and strode into the house, silently praying it wasn't too late.

Toby was standing in the hallway, wringing his hands. "What do you mean to do with her?" he asked, staring at the unconscious woman with a mixture of fear and fascination. "I thought the drawing room would be the wisest choice."

Marcus hesitated, seeing Toby's point. To take her upstairs would add to the scandal should word leak out, as he suspected it would, and yet she would be far more comfortable in a bed. It took him less than a second to make his choice. "I'm taking her upstairs," he said decisively, already turning toward the staircase. "Have Mrs. Leslie and one of the maids join me in the Blue Room, and then I want you to come up as well. I have an errand for you."

"Yes, Marcus." For once, Toby didn't argue but rushed off to do as he was bid.

Less than a minute later, Marcus was laying her on the pale blue counterpane, his eyes never leaving her face. She was still unconscious, but at least the bleeding had stopped, and beneath the blood he could see a gash just below her hairline. My God, he thought, his fingers trembling as he gently brushed the hair from the cut; the bastard must have used a cudgel on her. The realization filled him with white-hot fury, and his jaw clenched as he struggled for control. Blast Gilford, he cursed silently; if he ever got his hands on the young fool, he would snap his bloody neck!

He was debating whether or not he should remove her coat when the housekeeper bustled in, two maids bearing basins of water and rags trailing after her. "Mr. Flanders has told us everything, my lord," she said, gently but firmly shoving him aside as she took his place beside the bed. "Knocked down by a horse without so much as an I-beg-your-pardon! It makes a body wonder what this world is coming to!"

Marcus looked up, his eyes meeting the older woman's knowing gaze. A street accident was a weak explanation for Miss Portham's injuries, but it was far less scandalous than the truth. He gave an imperceptible nod and stepped back. "Thank you for coming so quickly, Mrs. Leslie," he said, favoring her with a grateful smile. "Now, if you'll excuse me, I must have a word with my cousin. I will be back in a moment." Without waiting for her answer, he walked out into the hall, where he found a very subdued Toby waiting for him.

"Upon my father's honor, I never meant for this to happen," he said, his brown eyes meeting Marcus's. "It was meant to be a joke, something to put me back in Julia's good graces. I never thought anyone would be hurt."

Marcus believed him at once, for despite his

self-absorbed foolishness, Toby had never been a truly malicious person. Not that that in any way diminished his responsibility, and the moment the danger was past, Marcus fully intended giving him sweet hell. Meanwhile there were more important tasks at hand.

"I am going to write a note to Lady St. Ives," he said, striding purposefully toward the library located across the hall from the guest suite. "You are to take it there at once and place it into her hands, and no other's. Is that understood?"

Toby paled and began licking his lips. "Lady St. Ives?" he repeated, his voice quavering. "Must I?"

"Considering Miss Portham may have been killed because of you, yes," Marcus replied curtly, refusing to feel pity for Toby's obvious reluctance.

"What if she's not there?" Toby asked, clinging to the faint hope. "What shall I do then?"

Marcus was already scribbling his urgent message on a piece of paper. "Then give it to Alex," he said, thinking he would welcome Alex's cool head. "And in the event he's not there, then return home. And Toby?" His cold eyes met Toby's as he handed him the letter.

"Yes?"

"If I find you have failed me in this, I will make you very, very sorry. Do you understand?"

Toby's heart plummeted to the soles of his Hessians. "Yes, my lord," he said in the accepting tones of a condemned man. "I understand perfectly."

She hurt. The thought intruded into the black mists swirling in Belle's head as she lay on the bed. She'd had migraines in the past, but never one so horribly painful. Her head felt as if it would explode, and her stomach was rolling with persistent nausea. She could hear faint sounds around her; Georgiana's voice, she thought, and Julia's tearful tones. She also thought she could hear a man's deep voice, and fretted that they'd evidently sent for a physician. Granted her migraine was bad, but that didn't mean she wanted some fool of a doctor dosing her with his heathenish potions. She was about to open her mouth and order him from the room when she heard a second voice speak.

"Lady St. Ives has just arrived with her husband. Do you wish her to wait below, or shall I have her brought up?"

Belle's brows puckered in confusion as she recognized Colford's deep voice. What the devil was he doing in her bedroom? she wondered with vague indignation. Moreover, why had her cousin allowed such a thing? Georgiana was usually such a stickler for propriety, and she could only conclude the arrogant devil had forced his way inside. Well, she decided proudly, they would just see about *that!*

She struggled to open her eyes, and was alarmed when they refused to cooperate. She tried again, her lashes fluttering as she slowly, painfully, opened her eyes. Her vision was cloudy at first, and it took several blinks for it to clear sufficiently for her to gaze about her. What on earth . . . Where was she?

"There now." The unfamiliar woman bending over her gave a warm smile. "Awake, are you? About time, miss. Gave us a devil of a fright, you did."

Belle could only stare at her, fighting her panic and confusion. It was like being a child again, waking in a new bed in a new house, and wondering how long she and her mama would be allowed to remain before being fobbed off on someone else. She wet her lips and spoke the first words to come to mind. "Where is my mother?"

"Oh heavens, her wits have been addled!" Georgiana cried, rushing forward to bend over the bed. "Dearest, dearest Belle, do you not know who I am?"

Belle winced, wishing she would lower her voice. "Yes, Georgiana, I do," she said, closing her eyes before she disgraced herself. "Would you kindly not jar the bed? It is making me quite ill."

Julia's tearstained face next appeared when Belle opened her eyes. "Oh, Cousin, thank heavens you are all right!" she cried, carrying Belle's limp hand to her cheek. "I have been so very frightened! When Jackson untied himself and came rushing in, we realized you'd been kidnapped, but we didn't know what to do! We were about to send for the runners when Mr. Gilford and Mr. Shipfield told us where you were."

Belle could only stare at her, wondering if indeed her wits had been addled, for none of what Julia said made the least bit of sense. And yet . . . In a rush it all came flashing back. The strange man on the carriage box, the new footman crowding behind her, and the pain that sent her hurtling into unconsciousness. She was trying to sort out the confusing whirl of images when she saw the earl standing just inside the room, and everything crystallized with amazing clarity.

"You wretch!" she exclaimed, trying to sit up on her elbows, only to be felled by the nausea and pain. She flopped back down on the bed and sent him an impotent glare. "You kidnapped me!"

"Belle!" Georgiana seemed shocked. "What a terrible thing to say! You must know it is simply not so!"

"Oh, must I?" Belle had never been so furious in

her life as she remembered her fear. "I'm here, aren't I?"

As there was no denying that, Georgiana gave an uncertain shrug. "Well, yes, I suppose you are, but—"

"I knew you were sailing in fairly deep waters, my lord," Belle interrupted with a sarcastic laugh, concentrating her fury on Colford, "but I had no idea you were quite so desperate as to resort to kidnapping!"

The earl stiffened, his expression wary as his gray eyes met hers. "I warn you, ma'am," he said, his voice controlled, "you had best be very sure of your facts before you make free with your accusations."

"Really? And what facts must I be sure of? The fact that your pockets are to let and you are desperate to make a marriage of convenience?" Belle demanded, a feeling of bitter betrayal washing over her. She'd always feared something like this would happen, but even when she and Colford were at daggers drawn, she'd never thought he would be the one to do it. In the past week she'd even grown to respect him, to like him, and this was how he repaid her. The pain of it was almost more than she could bear.

"Belle." The warning came from Pip, who had appeared in the doorway, her husband standing behind her. "Please, this isn't what you think."

"Isn't it?" Belle was furious to find she was close to tears. "Well, my lord, you needn't think it will work! I would not marry you were my name to be blackened from here to Land's End!"

There was a shocked gasp and then a stunned silence as everyone present held their breath. Lord Colford said nothing, but the fury on his harsh features was palpable as he stood in icy silence.

When he did speak, it was so softly that she had to strain to catch the words.

"And I, madam, would never marry you. I may be as poor as you say, but even if I hadn't a farthing to my name, I wouldn't be so desperate as to offer for an icicle like you. You may have more gold than I will ever hope to see, but that is all you have to offer a man." With that he whirled on his heel and left, brushing past Pip and the viscount without another word.

"Please, Miss Portham, will you not eat?" Annette implored, offering Belle another spoonful of beef broth the cook had prepared for her. "You'll never get back on you pins if you keep on this way!"

"No, thank you, Annette," Belle said tiredly, shuddering at the thought of food. "Later, perhaps, but not now. I would much rather rest."

Annette looked unconvinced. "I shall leave the bowl here," she said, placing it on the bedside table. "Mayhap you'll want some when you wake, hm?"

"Yes, yes, I am sure I shall," Belle promised, hoping it would incite the maid to leave. In the two days since the kidnapping, she'd been confined to her bed with a sore head and equally sore heart, and she wanted only to be left alone.

The young woman lingered several minutes, fluffing Belle's pillows and fussing over her until she thought she would scream. Finally she was gone, closing the door carefully behind her and leaving Belle alone with her unhappy thoughts.

How could she have done it? she wondered, not for the first time. How could she have made those hateful accusations to Colford? She would have liked to lay the blame on the bump on her head, but she knew that had little to do with it. It had been her own fear, her own distrust of the world, that had made her leap to the erroneous conclusion that the earl had been behind the kidnapping. Even as she'd been shouting at him, some small part of her had known she was wrong, and she wished now she had listened. Now it was too late.

After Colford had stormed out, everyone had begun talking at once. Georgiana had scolded her for ruining the family name, and Julia had wailed it was all her fault. The doctor was tutting about the effects of head wounds on one's sensibilities, and even Pip was lecturing her on her unbecoming behavior. Suddenly Mr. Flanders was there, his plump shoulders held back as he stood before her.

"You have grievously wronged my cousin, Miss Portham," he'd said in a surprisingly mature voice. "This whole contretemps is entirely my doing, and I sincerely ask your forgiveness. I only did it out of love for Julia, but if you wish it, I promise never to see her or you again."

Julia started wailing again, flinging herself into his arms and begging his forgiveness. Belle remembered staring at them, shamed and sickened as she realized what she'd done. In that moment she'd have given every pound she possessed to recall her bitter words, but instead she'd said nothing.

The rest of the afternoon was a blur, and she had only a vague memory of a strong footman carrying her out to her coach. Since then, she'd spent most of the time sleeping, tormented by nightmares of her parents' deaths and memories of the farcical kidnapping. In retrospect it seemed almost humorous, and she could only imagine Toby's dismay when he realized his doltish friends had carried off the wrong woman. It was probably just as well she'd been unconscious, she decided with a return of her old spirit. Had she been awake, she'd probably have boxed their ears and rung a peal over their head they'd not soon forget.

Despite her bleak thoughts, she managed to fall asleep, and when she next opened her eyes, she found the viscountess sitting at her bedside.

"Phillipa, what are you doing here?" she asked, wiping the sleep from her eyes like a drowsy child.

"Checking on you, of course." Pip's green eyes were filled with concern as she studied her friend's wan features. "Your cousin informs me you have sunk into a decline and are refusing to eat."

Belle flushed and glanced away. "It's rather difficult to eat when the room keeps swimming about you," she grumbled, kneading the bed sheets with her fingers. "I'll eat when I'm better."

"You'll eat now." Pip picked up the bowl from the table and scooped up a spoonful of tepid soup, proffering it to Belle with a menacing scowl.

Belle knew her friend too well to refuse, and managed to swallow the rest of the soup before Pip was satisfied. "There," the viscountess said, setting the bowl to one side. "Now, tell me, how are you feeling? Does your head still hurt?"

"Like the wrath of God," Belle admitted truthfully. "But it is getting better. I hope to be up by tomorrow."

"That is good." Pip nodded, although she was still scowling. "Just mind you don't rush things. Alex tells me head wounds can be quite dangerous."

"He would know," Belle answered, recalling the viscount had made his reputation as one of Wellington's bravest officers. "Speaking of Alex, how is he? Did your dinner go well? I cannot tell you how sorry I am to have missed it."

"No, you're not, for it was the most boring thing

you could imagine," Pip told her with a sigh. "Our guests were mostly Tories, and you know what a dull lot they are. Indeed, if it hadn't been for the gossip about your accident, the night should have been tedious beyond endurance."

"My accident?"

Pip nodded. "You were knocked down by a runaway horse in front of your house," she said, fixing Belle with a stern look. "The accident was witnessed by Alex and myself, and we carried you inside. Everyone was quite shocked and sympathetic, and it is agreed that the traffic in London is becoming a positive menace to public safety. The duke of Churchton means to raise the issue at the next debating session."

Belle managed a wan smile. "Yes, that sounds like something His Grace would do," she said, and then met the viscountess's gaze. "Pip, what about Colford? Is he all right?"

"Rather late to be worrying about that now, isn't it?"

The censure in her friend's voice hurt, but Belle told herself it was what she deserved. "Probably," she admitted quietly, "but I would still like to know. Was he there?"

"Yes, and I must say he handled himself quite well," Pip answered, then added, "Belle, how could you say such things? I've known you for eight years, and I've never known you to be so viciously cruel! How could you have thrown his debts into his face like that?"

Belle glanced away, fighting back tears. "I wish I knew," she said with painful honesty. "It wasn't just the bump on the head; it was . . . I don't know, so many things. I thought I'd been betrayed, and that Marcus had been the one to do it. I couldn't bear that, Pip, I couldn't."

Pip digested that, intrigued by Belle's confession

and the fact she'd referred to the earl by his given name. Knowing Belle's rigid sense of formality, Pip thought the slip highly significant. "Why should it hurt so much that it was Colford?" she asked, striving for indifference as she folded her arms across her chest. "I thought you couldn't abide the man."

Belle shrugged, still feeling perilously close to tears. "In the past weeks I have come to know him better, and I've decided he's not quite the villain I once took him for," she admitted. "In many ways he reminds me of Alex—both honorable and strong—and I know I have insulted him past all forgiveness. I only wish . . ."

"Wish what?"

"That I could make it up to him," Belle concluded, her eyes filled with misery as she met Pip's gaze. "I know he will accept my apology when I make it, but that still doesn't make it right. There *must* be something I can do to repay him."

"What?" Pip was intrigued.

"I don't know," Belle admitted, her jaw firming as her heart filled with resolve. "But I shall think of something, Pip. If it is the last thing I do, I shall think of something."

Seven

Julia and Georgiana were both cordial if somewhat cool when Belle appeared for breakfast the following morning. They were dressed to go out, and when Belle inquired as to their direction, Georgiana said, "We'd thought to call upon Lord Colford to formally offer him our thanks for his efforts on your behalf. We shall naturally understand if you choose not to join us."

"That is very good of you, Cousin." Belle forced herself to smile despite her pain. "It is probably best if I do not venture too far from home my first day out of the sickbed. However, I shall be writing his lordship a note conveying my thanks and my deepest apologies, and I trust you will deliver it for me."

Her calm request brought a confused scowl to Georgiana's face. "You are apologizing?" she asked, her brows meeting over her nose as she surveyed Belle.

"Mmm." She pretended to busy herself buttering her toast. "From what Pip said, I made a dreadful cake of myself, although truth to tell, I scarce remember any of it. I trust I didn't make a horrible scandal?"

Georgiana didn't know what to think. She'd been about to take the girl to task for her behavior, but she could hardly do that if she hadn't even been in her right mind. "You remember nothing?" she pressed suspiciously.

"Only that I was getting in my carriage one moment and fighting off attackers the next," Belle said, not untruthfully. "As I said, it is all very hazy, but I do recall waking up in a strange room and not knowing where I was. I asked for my mother, didn't I?"

"Yes," Georgiana replied slowly, thinking that perhaps she'd been a trifle hard on the poor child. "I thought you were all about in your head, and I didn't know what to do."

"Yes, that must have been it," Belle agreed with a nod. "You have figured it out exactly, ma'am. How clever of you."

"Yes, it is, rather." Georgiana preened. Of course Belle hadn't meant those awful words she had hurled at the earl, she decided complacently, raising her cup of tea to her lips. It was an accident. A knock on the head like that would be enough to rattle anyone.

"And how are you, dearest?" Belle next turned her attention to Julia, who'd remained silent through the exchange. "I hope you are recovered from your shock?"

"Yes, Cousin," Julia answered warily. Like Georgiana, she was more than willing to give her cousin the benefit of the doubt. "When Mr. Gilford and Mr. Shipfield first explained what happened, I fear I was quite out of charity with them. Still, all seems to have turned out well."

"Yes, Pip informs me that you and Mr. Flanders have mended your differences. Have you?" Belle nibbled at her eggs as she asked the question.

"We have." Julia's chin came up proudly as she faced Belle. "In fact, I have written Simon, telling him of my feelings, and I am sure once he knows my heart is engaged, he will give Toby permission to marry me."

Belle dredged up a casual shrug. "That is your choice, my dear, although I am sure you will understand if I am less than thrilled with the gentleman at the moment."

Julia blushed prettily and averted her eyes. "Yes, well, that was rather naughty of him," she conceded, toying with her fork. "But I read him a dreadful scold, and he has promised never to do anything like that again."

"That is reassuring. Does this mean I can safely traverse our city streets without fear of being carried off like one of the Sabine women?"

"Belle!"

"Cousin!"

It seemed neither Julia nor Georgiana appreciated Belle's wry humor, and she quickly hid a grin. "I was only asking," she said, striving for an innocent expression. "After what happened, you cannot blame me for wondering."

"What happened was a most unfortunate incident," Georgiana said, fixing Belle with a stern scowl. "That it hasn't yet landed us in the scandal broth is nothing short of miraculous, and I think it would be best if you refrained from mentioning it again. *Ever*," she added, lest Belle fail to take her meaning.

"Yes, Georgiana," Belle murmured, deciding for the moment that discretion was the better part of valor.

The tactic worked, and they were able to continue the rest of the meal in relative peace. Despite their concern over Belle, Julia and Georgiana had attended a ball the previous night, hoping it would help stave off rumors in the event that neither Mr. Gilford nor Mr. Shipfield could be trusted to hold their tongues. They left early, of course, and much to their relief, no one in the *ton* seemed any the wiser.

"Oh, that reminds me," Georgiana said, as she was finishing her tea. "The marquess of Berwick asked after you. He seemed quite upset when he heard of your accident, and asked if he might pay you a visit. I said I'd let him know when you were better."

"That was good of him," Belle said, thinking that his lordship had been paying her a great deal of attention of late. She was beginning to suspect he was courting her, and she wondered how far she should let it progress before gently hinting him away. She'd learned early it was best to nip such things in the bud, before the gentleman involved became overly confident.

Following breakfast, Belle quietly excused herself and retired to her study to write her apology. After several frustrating attempts, she gave up, realizing a prettily worded plea for forgiveness wouldn't suit. Much as she dreaded it, she knew the only honorable solution was to face Colford and personally apologize for her spiteful words. Once she admitted that, the rest was surprisingly easy, and she quickly penned a strained request that he call upon her at his earliest convenience. She only hoped he'd forgiven her enough to accept.

"Colford? I was wondering if I might have a word with you."

Marcus glanced up from his morning paper to find Toby standing in the doorway, his plump face set in the solemn lines he was beginning to recognize. Since the kidnapping, his heir had matured beyond all recognition, and while Marcus deplored the means, he could not fault the results. At last Toby seemed to be taking life, and himself, seriously.

"Certainly, Toby," he replied, setting his paper aside with a smile. "What is it? Are Mrs. Larksdale and Miss Dolitan early?"

"No, it's not that," Toby said, advancing into the library with a purposeful stride. "They will be here shortly, however, and I thought it would be best to have this matter settled between us before they arrive."

"I see," Marcus said, thrusting a hand through his hair and brushing the dark red locks back from his forehead. "That sounds rather ominous. May I ask what it is we are settling?"

Toby lowered himself onto the red leather club chair facing Marcus. "I have been thinking," he began carefully, "and I've decided I want more from life than to sit about waiting for a pair of dead man's shoes. No offense intended, my lord," he added with an anxious look.

"None taken," Marcus assured him, amused by Toby's concern. "I'm well aware you are my heir and will inherit should anything happen to me."

"Thing of it is, sir, when I was free ... that is, not engaged to be married, living 'pon my expectations was fine. But now that I'm to be wed, I realize I shall need to provide for my wife and family, and I really cannot do that standing about waiting for you to catch a chill."

Marcus reached up to rub his chin, taking care to hide the shock he felt at Toby's blunt confession. In the past year he'd dropped any number of hints that Toby take over one of the few remaining estates, only to have his hints ignored. That he was now pressing for such responsibilities was indeed encouraging.

"What did you have in mind?" he asked, already reviewing the possibilities in his mind.

Toby ran a nervous finger around the collar of his neckcloth. "Actually, Julia had a suggestion I thought rather interesting. Her cousin has a small farm in Surrey that she has promised to Julia, and I thought we might live there. It's small, as I say, but with careful management—"

"No."

Toby frowned at Marcus's curt response. "Well, I don't mean to manage it myself," he said, obviously offended. "There's already a capable fellow there, and I see no reason to replace him. Besides, I shall be too busy writing to worry about soil and all that other rot."

"I said no!" Marcus snapped, his eyes flashing silver as he leapt to his feet. "You're not taking a damned thing from that woman, and that is final!"

For once, Toby understood Marcus without further explanation. "I know you're still hipped with Miss Portham, and can't say as I blame you," he said with newfound maturity. "But all of that is beside the point. I wasn't asking your permission, my lord, I was informing you of my plans."

Marcus flushed with mortification and resumed his seat. "I didn't mean to snap," he said, selecting his next words with care. "It is just that I don't feel it's necessary for you and your bride to live off Miss Portham's generosity. Granted our holdings have been depleted over the past few years, but we aren't yet reduced to penury. The estate outside of York is almost free of debt. Perhaps you and Julia could settle there?"

"Thought of that," Toby answered calmly, "but we decided it is too far from the city. Julia wishes to be near her brother and Miss Portham, and I would like to be close enough to pop into town to meet with my publisher and other writers."

"Your publisher?"

"Didn't I tell you?" Toby preened with pleasure.

"I sold some of my poems to a publisher who is interested in seeing more of my work. Not a great deal of money, but a start. I shall dedicate my first volume to Julia, of course."

"Of course," Marcus echoed, shamed as he recalled his indifferent dismissal of Toby's work. "Congratulations, Toby; I am very proud of you."

"I'm using my own name," Toby admitted, feeling greatly daring. "Scribbling's respectable now that Byron has come along, so you needn't think anyone will object. Although I shall take a nom de plume if I decide to write a novel," he added, lest his very proper cousin take exception.

"Whatever pleases you," Marcus replied, vowing to be more understanding of Toby's ambitions. "In the meanwhile, I wish you'd reconsider your decision to live at Miss Dolitan's farm. I would not have you accused of marrying her for her money."

"Posh, what do I care for tattle?" Toby dismissed Marcus's words with an indifferent shrug. "Besides, wasn't you telling me only a few months ago that we'd have to make an advantageous marriage if we was to save Colford?"

The novelty of having Toby throw his own words back in his face wasn't at all to Marcus's liking. "I said *I* would have to make an advantageous marriage," he corrected with an embarrassed grumble, the tips of his ears growing red. "I didn't mean you were expected to sacrifice yourself for the estate."

"Rot, you said quite clearly that instead of languishing after fashionable impures, I ought to devote myself to obtaining a well-dowered bride! You said 'twas my duty to bring a bit of money into the family coffers instead of squandering it."

Marcus slumped lower in his chair, his chagrin increasing as he recalled the conversation. He'd just finished meeting with his solicitor, and he'd been feeling rather grim. The bill for a new bonnet for Toby's *chéri ami* had been the final straw, and he'd lashed out at the younger man. At the time he'd felt justified in his anger, but now he was aware of a strong feeling of distaste. He heaved a gusty sigh, his eyes closing in weariness. "Toby, I—"

"Besides," Toby interrupted, "it's not as if Julia was as wealthy as her cousin. I could see your objections then. Dashed awkward marrying so wealthy a lady ... unless one's pockets were just as deep," he added with a thoughtful frown.

Marcus's expression grew even bleaker. "Yes," he said at last, "unless one was of equal wealth, such a marriage would be most awkward."

"Well, there you are." Toby nodded wisely. "But since Julia ain't an heiress like Miss Portham, there's no reason why we shouldn't accept her offer." When Marcus didn't respond, he leaned closer. "Come, my lord, if Julia wasn't related to The Icicle, you'd have no objections to our living there, would you?"

The appearance of the butler announcing guests spared Marcus the necessity for answering, but the question was much on his mind during the visit. Both Mrs. Larksdale and Julia were profuse in their gratitude, thanking him again and again for all he'd done for Belle.

"Naturally she is most appreciative, but unfortunately she still isn't able to venture out of the house," Georgiana said, extracting the letter Belle had given her from her reticule and handing it to the earl. It had been sealed with a circlet of red wax, which prevented her from stealing a peek at its contents, vexing her no end. "She asked that I give you this."

Marcus accepted the letter quietly, keeping his

expression controlled as he scanned the missive.
When he was finished he refolded it and tucked it
into the inside pocket of his green velvet jacket.
He could see the curiosity on their faces, but remained stubbornly closemouthed. Instead he
turned to Julia, his manner friendly as he asked if
she'd written her brother.

"Yes, but of course, it is far too early to expect a
reply," she answered, nervously slipping her hand
into Toby's comforting clasp. "Would—would you
like his direction, my lord?"

"That is an excellent idea, Miss Dolitan," he told
her with a warm smile. "As Toby's nearest male
relation, I suppose it shall fall to me to assure him
that Toby's intentions are honorable. Are they
puppy?" He shot Toby a teasing look.

"Most honorable, my lord," Toby assured him,
carrying Julia's hand to his lips for a brief kiss.

They continued chatting pleasantly, and all too
soon it seemed the ladies took their leave. Toby accompanied them to their carriage, and the moment
the door closed behind them, Marcus took the letter from his pocket and reread it.

> *My Lord,*
> *I know you must hate me, and after all that I
> have said and done, I cannot find it in my heart to
> blame you. My words, like my actions, are beyond
> forgiveness, and I will not insult you by asking for
> that which I so clearly do not deserve.*
>
> *I would, however, request you call upon me at
> my house this afternoon so that I might make my
> apologies as I made my hateful and untrue accusa-
> tions, in your presence. It is the only way I can
> possibly hope to atone for what I have done, and I
> humbly ask you to grant me this favor.*
> *Sincerely,*
> *Arabelle Portham*

Marcus returned the letter to his pocket, his expression harsh as his pride waged war with his conscience. On the one hand he told himself it would be better for all concerned if he mended his fences with Miss Portham. It seemed certain Toby and Miss Dolitan would be making a match of it, and he'd learned long ago that it never did for families to be at odds with each other. Besides, after the two young lovers were wed, it was unlikely he and Miss Portham would need to see much of each other. He need only suffer her company for a few weeks, and then they would never see each other again, except socially.

On the other hand, he reminded himself grimly, she'd called him a fortune hunter. She'd thrown his debts in his face and then accused him of the most heinous crime imaginable. How could he possibly forgive her for that?

He was no closer to resolving his painful dilemma when Toby returned, accompanied by Lord St. Ives.

"I thought I'd find you here," Alex said, greeting him with a smile. "Have you forgotten the opposition is debating today? We'll need to hurry if we mean to be there in time to hiss and shout them down as befits a proper Tory."

His friend's teasing words brought a reluctant grin to Marcus's face. "For shame, sir, you know we Tories are beyond such base behavior," he drawled, attempting to match Alex's lighthearted tones. "I fear your lady wife has had a detrimental effect upon your reasoning, to say nothing of your party loyalties."

"Indubitably, but you did warn me how it would be when I set out to marry her," Alex replied, the fatuous look on his face making it obvious he was more than satisfied with the situation.

Toby shifted uneasily. All this talk of Lady St. Ives reminded him of last year's unpleasantness, and his own innocent role in the scandal. Much as he would have liked to creep from the room, Toby decided it was time to pay the piper. Now that he was an engaged man, it was time he began standing up for himself. He nervously cleared his throat

"My lord, I was wondering if I might say something."

St. Ives glanced up, surprised by the solemn note in Toby's voice. "Certainly, Flanders," he said pleasantly. "What is it?"

"It was most improper of me to embroil you in that foolish wager last year," Toby said, standing ramrod-straight. "I had no right to drag Miss Lambert's name through scandal by betting you couldn't get her to attend the prince's ball with you, and I ask that you forgive me."

His words shocked both Alex and Marcus, and they exchanged startled looks. "You admit . . . finally that you were wrong?" Alex was the first to recover from his surprise.

"Yes, your lordship." Toby was determined to make a clean breast of it. "And I am sorry I brought that snake Kingsford into it as well, although I had nothing to do with his locking you and Miss Lambert in your bedchamber. Dashed bad show, that."

"Not really." After a year, Alex could look back upon the incident without wanting to kill the young lord and his vicious sister, who had lured Pip to his room under false pretenses. "And if one may quote the Bard: 'All's well that ends well.' "

"Perhaps, but I wish you to know that I sincerely regret the incident," Toby said, pleased at how well the viscount was taking his apology. Perhaps he could make it through the Season without the viscount putting a bullet through him after all, he thought with a flash of optimism.

Alex and Marcus exchanged another look. "Apology accepted, Flanders," Alex said, rising to his feet to offer Toby his hand. "Now, let us speak no more of the matter. Hmm?"

"Yes, my lord." Toby eagerly accepted the other man's hand. Evidently there was much to recommend responsibility, he decided with a flash of newfound insight.

"By the by, Flanders, I hear congratulations are in order," Alex said, once he had resumed his seat. "May I wish you and the young lady happy?"

"Yes, my lord, you may," Toby said proudly. "Mr. Dolitan ain't given his permission just yet, so we can't be posting the banns, but we're hopeful he will give us the nod."

"Yes, I am sure you are," Alex answered with a look in his dark blue eyes that made Toby wonder if perhaps he had been too hasty in his relief. "But first a word of advice to you, Flanders, if I may."

"Advice?" Toby swallowed the sudden lump in his throat.

"Take care not to embroil your fiancée in any of your silly wagers. I should hate to see Miss Dolitan's good name bandied about as was my wife's only last year. Her honor is your honor now, and vice versa. See that you remember that."

Toby stuttered a promise to guard Julia's name with his life, and then fled from the room, leaving Marcus to shake his head at the viscount.

"There was no need to terrorize the lad," Marcus chided with a reproving look. "I told you, I'd already given him a severe dressing down for his part in that farce, and he's had nothing to do with Kingsford since. He is reformed."

"Perhaps." Alex dismissed Toby with a cool

shrug. "Although I hold with the old saw that leopards seldom change their spots, and if this last stunt is any indication, our young kit has a spot or two left that bears watching. I can't believe we managed to avoid scandal ... again. The gods must be smiling on us."

Marcus thought of the letter in his pocket. "Alex, may I ask you something?"

"What?"

Marcus hesitated, not certain what to say. Alex had been present when Miss Portham had made her accusations, and although he'd never referred to them again, he could not help but wonder if he agreed with at least part of what she had said. "Do you think I am a fortune hunter?" he asked, his gray eyes meeting Alex's blue gaze. "The truth, if you please."

Alex raised a dark eyebrow, but other than that small outward sign, he managed to hide the severity of the shock he'd been dealt. He remained silent, debating on whether to be truthful or tactful, but in the end he knew only the truth could stand between them. Drawing a deep breath, he faced Marcus squarely.

"Since last year, you have been open with me about your need to make a profitable marriage," he said, his deep voice even, "so in that respect I suppose you could be labeled a fortune hunter. However," he added when Marcus would have turned away, "most fortune hunters lack your integrity and decency. Rather than being honest about their intentions, they disguise them behind words of love, offering sweet promises of affection only to betray their luckless wives once the money is safely in their control. That is something you would never do, and so no, I would have to say that you are not a fortune hunter."

"Then what the devil am I?" Marcus demanded, his voice strained with emotion.

"An honorable man who will do whatever it takes to protect his family and his name," Alex said calmly, stepping forward to lay a comforting hand on his shoulder. "I do not fault you for that, Marcus, nor in her heart does Miss Portham."

"You sound certain of that," Marcus answered with a bitter laugh, remembering her fiery anger as she'd shouted at him.

"I am," Alex replied, wishing he could tell Marcus what Pip had told him in confidence the night of the kidnapping. Perhaps if he knew of Miss Portham's early life, he would understand the pain behind her angry words.

"She is much like my Pip in that regard," he said instead, cautiously sharing with Marcus what he could. "The nature they show the world is but a sham designed to protect them from the cruelty of others." When Marcus still looked unconvinced, he added, "You have come to know Miss Portham rather well these past few weeks; is she really The Icicle you once named her?"

A hundred images filled Marcus's head. Images of Miss Portham riding in the park, her golden eyes sparkling with affection as she teased Julia; or Miss Portham dressed in a stunning ball gown, her blond hair wisping about her face as she defiantly faced him across a stone balcony. She was a warm, vital, beautiful woman, and as far removed from an icicle as it was possible to be. He realized with a sinking heart that he'd ceased thinking her as one a very long time ago, and the realization brought a fresh flash of pain.

"No," he said, turning away from Alex's too-seeing gaze. "She is not."

"Then when she apologizes, you will accept?"

Marcus discreetly raised one hand to touch the letter lying against his heart. "I will accept," he said, the words sounding as empty and as cold as his soul.

Eight

"Go to the theater while you remain home alone? Nonsense, Belle, I could never be so cruel!" Julia's soft blue eyes were filled with reproach as she studied her cousin. They had just finished tea and were discussing how to spend the evening. Georgiana was set for a few hands of Pope Joan, while Julia was looking forward to a quiet night of reading. It never occurred to either lady to leave the invalid to her own devices, and they were shocked by the very suggestion.

"Indeed, we could never consider such a thing," Georgiana added with a disapproving frown. "Whatever would people say?"

"Very little, I should imagine," Belle replied wearily, reaching up to rub her temple. The lump had subsided, leaving a garish bruise which stood out like a brand against her pale skin. "Besides," she continued crossly, "the two of you went out last night, and no one seemed to mind. Why should tonight be any different?"

Georgiana gave a loud sigh and fixed Belle with a sagacious look. "To go out one evening while one has a relation who is convalescing may be excused as a necessity," she said in the long-suffering tones of a parent afflicted with a dull-witted child. "To go out two evenings in a

121

row, however, would be construed as dereliction of one's familial duty, and that I cannot allow. We shall remain at home."

Belle closed her eyes, fighting the desire to engage in a noisy bout of the vapors. Her nerves felt strained to the breaking point, and she wanted nothing more than to be left alone to brood. Surely there had to be some way she could convince her well-meaning relations to leave, she thought, her mind whirling with possible solutions. Then it came to her.

"I'm sure you know what's best," she said, assuming a meek air. "And I admit I would welcome your company. It is only . . ."

"Only what?" Georgiana demanded when she did not complete the sentence. "Speak up, gel!"

"It is only that I feel it would be best for you to go to the theater as planned," Belle replied, mentally crossing her fingers. "You must know if you remain at home, it will cause even more speculation. I daresay by tomorrow evening it will be all over London that I am at death's door. Why else would you have missed the performance unless I was grievously injured?"

Georgiana sat back in her chair, her brows pleating as she ruminated. "I suppose you are right," she said with obvious reluctance. "Your absence has already elicited a great deal of tattle, and if both Julia and I were to show up missing, people would likely assume the worse."

Belle had to hide a smile at the note of shocked disapproval in her cousin's voice. "Yes, it is appalling the way some people leap to conclusions," Belle said primly, praying she wasn't overplaying her hand. "Still, I daresay we could weather the storm with our reputations more or less intact. And once I am seen out and about, everyone will know it was all a hum."

"Yes, but in the meanwhile what damage will be done to your good name ... and Julia's?" Georgiana asked rhetorically. "No, I see no hope for it. We shall have to go to the theater."

"And to the Drinkwater's dinner afterwards," Belle reminded them, recalling the invitation. "We've already accepted, and it would be most ill bred not to appear. Think of the wasted food."

"That is so," Georgiana acknowledged with another frown. "And it would be just like that dreadful Louella to put the worst possible interpretation on it, too. I cannot think why you agreed to attend, Belle. You must know I do not like that woman above half!"

"I am sorry, Cousin," Belle answered, judiciously refraining from reminding the other woman that she had accepted the invitation only at her behest, and that at the time she'd proclaimed the countess to be her "dearest friend."

"Can't be helped, I suppose," Georgiana grumbled, rising to her feet. "Well, if we're going to be up until dawn, I'd best lie down for a bit. You, too, young lady," she said to Julia. "It won't do for you to go about looking all pale and hollow-eyed. People will think Belle contagious."

"Yes, Cousin," Julia replied demurely, but remained seated. "But first I should like to discuss some things with Belle."

Georgiana nodded her approval and departed, leaving Belle and Julia alone. After a few uncomfortable seconds, Julia said, "Are you certain you don't mind being left alone? I feel terrible going off and leaving you with no one but the servants."

"I shall be fine, dearest," Belle assured her, feeling a twinge of guilt at deceiving the girl. "In fact, I'll probably be in bed by the time you leave. My head is still rather painful."

Julia looked alarmed. "Do you think we ought to send for the doctor?"

Belle shook her head, and then winced at the jolt of pain. "No, no, I am fine so long as I remember not to do things like *that*," she added, gingerly touching her head. "I am just pampering myself so that I shall be recovered in time for your coming-out ball next week."

"That is what I wished to discuss with you," Julia said, her voice hesitant. "Toby and I were hoping you would allow us to announce our engagement at the ball. Simon will be there, as well as our other relations, and we thought it would be the perfect opportunity. With your approval, that is." And she cast her an anxious look.

Belle swallowed her protest, knowing that ultimately Julia's life was her own. However much she might disapprove of the match, it was not her place to pass judgment. She'd already done that once this week, she reminded herself glumly, and only look at where it had landed her.

"The ball is in your honor, Julia," she said gently, leaning forward to take her hand. "You may do whatever you like. And I quite agree with you that it would be the perfect place to announce your engagement. But don't you think you ought to wait to hear from Simon before saying anything? It would be most awkward if he were to withhold his approval of the marriage."

"Oh, he will approve." Julia was confident in her brother's love. "I adore Toby with all my heart, and he loves me. That will matter far more to Simon than mere position or money."

Belle flushed at Julia's unspoken implication that such considerations mattered to her. "Still, I prefer that you wait until he has given you his blessing," she said firmly. "Once he has done that, you may announce it to whomever you please."

"Thank you, dearest Belle!" Julia leapt to her feet and deposited a kiss on Belle's cheek. "And Simon will give us his approval, I know he will!"

She departed in a flurry of silk, and Belle poured herself another cup of tea, then sat back to reflect upon her conversation with Julia. Did she put position and money above all else? she wondered, her heart sinking as she considered the possibility. She hated to think she could be so mercenary, yet she feared she had done precisely that.

The admission hurt, and Belle blinked back the tears that were pooling in her eyes. It was ironic that she who had spent most of her life being judged by her pocketbook should then use that same measuring stick on the rest of the world. It was beyond hypocrisy, and she hated herself for succumbing to the false values that had often caused her such suffering.

No wonder Marcus refused to forgive her, she decided, wiping the tears from her cheek with a trembling hand. It had been hours since Julia and Georgiana had returned home, and still there had been no word from him. She hadn't expected him to come rushing straight over, of course, but she had hoped he'd respond by the end of the day. Now she would have to wait until tomorrow . . . if she was lucky, she added with an unhappy sigh.

Several hours later she was in the drawing room enjoying the peace and solitude when Gibson appeared, his face set in lines of rigid disapproval. "I beg your pardon, Miss Portham," he said, executing a stiff bow. "Lord Colford has called and is asking to see you. I have placed him in the salon."

Belle's heart began pounding at the news. She'd all but given up hope up hearing from him, and relief made her giddy. Relief and another emotion she dared not name. She glanced down at her gown, wincing when she saw its wrinkled state. She simply couldn't appear in front of the earl looking like this, she realized unhappily, and rose quickly to her feet.

"Pray tell his lordship I will be with him in a few minutes," she replied, turning toward the door. When the butler remained steadfast, she gave him a quizzical look. "Is something amiss?"

Gibson sent her a reproving look. "As your cousins are both absent from the house, I have taken the liberty of instructing that the salon door be kept open," he said, his tone letting it be known he would brook no opposition. "Also, Mrs. Ponds will be seated just outside should you"—he paused delicately—"require anything."

Belle grew red at this reminder that an unmarried lady never entertained gentlemen without a chaperon of some sort present. If she'd been thinking at all, she would have arranged to meet him in a more public place.

"Thank you, Gibson," she said, flashing him a grateful smile. "I knew I could count upon your discretion. Now, if you'll pardon me, I must see to my gown. Pray see to his lordship's comfort."

What could be keeping her? Marcus wondered, pulling his watch from his pocket and studying it with a frown. The butler had assured him Miss Portham hadn't retired, so why had he been kept cooling his heels for the better part of a quarter hour? At this rate the play would be half-over before he even arrived. He was considering ringing for the footman to demand word of his hostess when the door opened and she stepped inside.

She looked even smaller, somehow, and infinitely more beautiful. She was wearing a dress of bronze jaconet, her hair arranged in soft curls about her face. It was the first time he'd seen her with her hair down, and as his eyes rested on her, he wondered what it would feel like to bury his hands in the shimmering golden waves.

"I am pleased that you came," Belle said, her hand held out as she advanced toward him. Her knees were shaking, and she prayed she wouldn't disgrace herself by collapsing at his feet. "I wasn't sure if you would."

He took her hand in his, noting with concern how cool it felt. "I would have been here sooner, but the speeches took longer than we expected. You know how long-winded the Whigs can be once you get them started." These words were offered with a teasing smile that elicited a slow smile in return.

"I shall say nothing, my lord, although I would urge that you not repeat that bon mot in front of Lady St. Ives," she said, tipping back her head to gaze up at him. "I fear she would disagree most strenuously."

"So St. Ives has already warned me," he answered, awed again by her sheer beauty. In the flickering light of the candles her skin glowed like the rarest of pearls, warm and inviting to the touch, and it was all he could do not to reach out and sample its softness for himself. A stray curl lay across her forehead, and unable to resist the temptation, he raised his hand to brush it back. Then he froze.

"Oh, my God!"

"What?" Belle's hand fluttered up, only to be stayed by his. He held her fingers in a gentle grip while his other hand tenderly brushed back the hair from her temple, revealing the bruise and the still-healing cut.

A soundless oath formed on his lips as he squeezed his eyes shut. "I am sorry, Belle," he said, using her first name without conscious thought. "I am so sorry."

Belle trembled beneath his touch, her heart melting at the self-loathing she saw stamped on his ashen face. "Why should you be sorry?" she asked, using his grip on her fingers to carry his hand to her cheek. "You did nothing wrong, Marcus. *Nothing*. That is why I asked to see you. I wanted to tell you that I—"

"I could have killed Gilford," he said, his gaze holding hers. "I wanted to, and had I known how badly he'd hurt you, I would have."

The soft violence in his voice convinced her he meant every word. "You would have had to wait until I had my chance at him," she said, striving for lightness even as her senses were swimming at his nearness. His fingers were lazily brushing over her cheek, and she lacked the will to move away. Later, she promised herself silently, her breath catching in her throat. Later.

As an experienced man of the world, Marcus sensed her response, and it filled him with a rush of masculine pleasure. He wanted to taste her sweet lips more than he wanted to draw his next breath, and for a wild moment he considered saying to hell with his conscience and doing just that. He bent his head closer, his fingers tightening on her jaw, and the action made the letter rustle in his pocket. The sound penetrated his inflamed senses, snapping him out of his trance as nothing else would have done. He released her abruptly, swinging away and silently cursing himself for his lack of honor.

He stared down unseeingly at the flames dancing in the grate, his hands clenching in a tight fist. "It would seem your fears about me were right, Miss Portham," he said, his voice as tight as the control he was exerting over himself. "I am apparently not to be trusted where you are concerned."

Belle could only gaze at him, confused and dazed by turns. She'd never felt such emotions in her life, and she wasn't sure if she could deal with the wildness they invoked. Waging her own battle for control, she managed to draw a deep breath.

"No," she said quietly, her chin coming up with pride. "I was wrong to say such things. I know you would never do anything to bring disgrace on either my good name or yours. You are much too honorable for that."

Marcus almost laughed, wondering if she had any idea how close she'd come to losing a great deal more than her good name. Even though they hadn't even kissed, his passions were inflamed, and the strength of that passion left him aching with need. "You seem to swing between extremes, Miss Portham," he said with a self-deprecatory smile. "You need to learn moderation, for that is where the truth lies. I am neither saint nor sinner, I am simply a man."

And I am a woman, she longed to scream, although shyness and fear held her silent. She wondered what he would do if she were to say the provocative words, and then decided she couldn't take the risk. If he turned around and she saw pity in his eyes, something inside her would surely die. She bit her lip and reached deep down inside of herself for the cool self-possession that had served her so well in the past.

"I am aware of that, my lord," she said evenly, relaxing as she felt the comforting shell of ice forming about her. "And it is to that man I wish to make my apologies. I said terrible things to him, things which I knew to be a lie even as I was saying them, and I am hoping he will find it in himself to forgive me. Do you think he will?"

He could sense the coolness in her voice, even as he heard the sincerity of her words, and knew without turning around that she had retreated behind her facade. Part of him was tempted to whirl around and take her in his arms, melting that facade so thoroughly that she would never be able to erect it again. The other part of him knew that if he did that, he would never let her go, and the admission made him clench his teeth in pain. He took a steadying breath before turning around to meet her gaze.

"I am sure he will," he replied, not trusting himself to touch her again. "And as I recall, he said some rather horrible and untrue things himself. Is it too much to hope he has also been forgiven?"

The shell encasing Belle cracked slightly. "Perhaps he wasn't far from wrong," she said, her voice shaking. "Perhaps all I have to offer a man is my money. It is all anyone else has ever wanted from me."

The pain in her voice drew him forward to lay both hands on her slender shoulders. "He was an ass," he told her firmly, ducking his head to meet her troubled eyes. "Then and all those years ago when he called you by that unforgivable name. He was an ill-mannered, bitter young man full of champagne and himself, and you were right to slap his face."

"But I—"

"No, Belle," he interrupted, knowing the time had come to make a full apology. "There are no excuses for my actions that night, none at all. Only know that I have regretted them ever since, and if there was any way I could undo the damage, I would gladly do it. You are a lady, and I cannot apologize enough for forgetting that."

His heartfelt apology for that night was almost Belle's undoing. She'd long ago recovered from her original anger over the incident, and although the name he had given her occasionally stung, she had come to take a macabre pride in it. She had even done her best to encourage her reputation as an Ice Maiden, using the image to keep the rest of the world at arm's length. Knowing that, she felt like the worst sort of hypocrite, listening to his words of self-loathing, and she knew she couldn't allow him to continue blaming himself. She ducked her head and turned away. "My lord, there is something I—"

"How long have we known each other?"

Of all the replies she might have expected, that wasn't one of them, and she glanced back over her shoulder. "I beg your pardon?"

"How long have we known each other?" he repeated, enjoying the puzzled look on her face.

"I am not sure," she said, wondering what he was hinting at. "Seven years, I suppose, perhaps eight. Why?"

"Then we're not strangers?"

"Of course not! But I fail to see what that has to do—"

"A moment ago, before we had resolved our differences, you called me Marcus," he explained, his hands coming up to turn her gently around. "If you could extend that courtesy to a man who was your enemy, could you not do the same for me?"

She colored brightly, unable to meet his gaze. "I never regarded you as an enemy," she grumbled.

He smiled at the top of her head. "Didn't you?" he asked provocatively. "Well, no matter. We are friends now—at least I hope we are—and I should like you to call me Marcus, as all my friends do."

"All your friends?" Lady Bingington's smiling countenance danced in front of Belle's eyes.

"Most of them," he corrected, savoring the slight note of jealousy in her voice. "The others call me

Colford, which you might also do, if it pleases you."

That sounded acceptable to Belle, and she raised her head again. "Very well ... Colford," she said, noting for the first time the green and gold flecks in his light gray eyes. "And as a friend, may I ask you a question?"

"Of course."

"Do you always go about collecting your apologies dressed to the nines?"

At first Marcus couldn't understand her meaning, and then he remembered his attire. "Ah, you mean this." His hands lifted as he held his arms out at his side. "I was on my way to the theater when I stopped to see you. Which reminds me, I had best be on my way, else my party will think I have forgotten her."

"Ah, you are referring to Lady Bingington." Belle managed a wise nod. "Well, I shouldn't worry if I were you. Although I am not well acquainted with Her Grace, I am told she is possessed of a most understanding nature. I am sure that once you explain your long-winded Tories to her, she will forgive your tardiness."

"Whigs," Marcus corrected, wondering now if he'd imagined that jealous note in her voice, and wondering also why it should matter. "It was the long-winded Whigs that delayed my arrival."

Belle's impish smile hid the pain eating at her. "My mistake, Colford. Now, hurry off before you miss the ovations. I hear Kean is doing Hamlet. You wouldn't want to miss *that*."

The next morning Belle was up and about long before her cousins were stirring. Even though she'd retired shortly after Marcus had taken his leave, she was still awake when Julia and Georgiana had returned shortly before three. She was bleary-eyed from lack of sleep, but she wasn't about to let that keep her from her appointments. She'd received a rather urgent missive from Mrs. Langston regarding Amanda Perryvale, and she wanted to make sure all was well with the little girl.

The children were in their classrooms when she arrived at the Academy, and there was no one about as she slipped into the headmistress's study. She surprised the good lady enjoying a quiet cup of tea, and waved aside her stammering apologies with a smile.

"You needn't think I intend you to slave from sunup to sundown, Mrs. Langston," she said as she took her seat before the desk. "In fact, a cup of tea sounds utterly delightful. Is there enough for me, do you think?"

"Of course there is!" the headmistress exclaimed, shaking her head and muttering to herself as she poured Belle a steaming cup of the fragrant beverage. When she was sure her benefactress had all she required, she settled back in her own chair.

"I am so glad to see you have recovered from your accident," she said, studying Belle anxiously. "I was worried when I heard you'd been run down. And in front of your own house, too! 'Tis a miracle you weren't killed!"

"It wasn't quite so serious as all that," Belle said, hating the need to continue the deception. "A horse bolted from its owner, and I was knocked down when it brushed past me."

"That's what comes from letting those foolish young men keep their rag-mannered nags in town," Mrs. Langston pronounced with a knowing nod. "It was only a matter of time before there was a tragedy. I knew it."

Belle took a hasty sip of tea, wondering if Mrs.

Langston was also possessed of prophetic bones. In the next minute she was dismissing the frivolous thought, focusing her attention on the reason behind her visit. "Mrs. Langston, you wrote there was a problem with Amanda Perryvale. What is it? I trust she hasn't fallen ill?"

"Oh heavens, no!" Mrs. Langston looked horrified at the very suggestion. "This is a modern academy! We should never allow our students to become *diseased!*"

"Then what is the problem?" Belle asked, gritting her teeth to control her impatience.

Mrs. Langston set her teacup aside with a sigh. "It is her uncle, or rather the man we think is her uncle, but who insists he is not. I fear he may bring action against us."

"What?" The teacup rattled precariously in Belle's hand. "Do you mean he has threatened us?"

"Yes, or at least his solicitor has. I received a letter yesterday stating that if we persist in our attempts to contact the duke, a charge of blackmail will be laid against us."

"Blackmail!" Bell was on her feet, her eyes flashing with fury. "How dare he accuse us of anything so monstrously untrue?"

"Well"—Mrs. Langston nervously cleared her throat—"it may have something to do with the letter Miss Pringle sent him."

"Miss Pringle?"

"One of our new teachers. I believe I may have mentioned her the last time you were here."

"Yes, I remember." Belle resumed her seat and picked up her teacup. "Thomasina Pringle, I believe you said?"

"Yes." Mrs. Langston nodded again. "A dear girl, and terribly sweet, but rather ... er ... determined when it comes to doing what she considers to be right. When the last letter she sent to His Grace imploring him to call upon Amanda was returned with a stern note insisting he had no niece, I fear she took it amiss, and she wrote a second letter threatening to reveal to the papers what she termed his callous indifference. The note from the solicitor arrived the following day."

Belle's eyes widened with dismay. "Oh dear," she said weakly, swallowing the lump in her throat.

"Yes, it is rather disconcerting," Mrs. Langston agreed. "I was hoping you might write His Grace a letter and assure him our reputation is above reproach. He hinted we did this sort of thing all the time," she added with an indignant sniff.

"Oh, did he?" Belle's anger stirred again. "In that case, I should be delighted to respond to him. May I see the letter, please?"

Mrs. Langston happily fetched the letter from her desk. "I am sure this is all a dreadful misunderstanding," she said, handing the missive to Belle. "Once cooler heads have prevailed, all will be smoothed out, and naturally I shall insure that Thomasina ceases her activities where Amanda is concerned."

"Ah yes, Miss Pringle," Belle replied, deciding she simply had to meet the other lady. "Where is she?"

"She is in her classroom." Mrs. Langston nervously bit her lip. "You're . . . you're not going to dismiss her, are you? She really is the dearest thing, and the children adore her."

"I shan't dismiss her," Belle promised, rising to her feet. "But I do intend having a word with her. I simply cannot have my teachers blackmailing our student's families."

She found Miss Pringle in a classroom surrounded by a group of children who were listening wide-eyed as she read from the book cradled in her hands.

" '. . . awful specter. Dark it was, and writhing and moaning as if in mortal pain. Esmerelda took a tremulous step closer, the torch she held clutched in her hand provided but a meager light that scarce pierced the shadowy darkness of the secret chamber. She advanced closer, closer, drawn as if by an unseen tether. Suddenly one of the shadows detached itself from the wall, its clawed hands reaching out as Esmerelda, innocent of the danger, passed within its reach. Just as she passed its cave, a scream rang out and . . .' There, I believe that is where we shall stop today." And she closed the book with a snap.

"Oh, Miss Pringle, no!" one young lady cried, lowering the hands that were shielding her face to cast her teacher a pleading look. "You can't stop there! What happens next?"

"You shall just have to wait and see," Miss Pringle said, her hazel eyes sparkling behind the lenses of her wire-rimmed glasses. "And you all know what the payment will be, don't you?"

"Four pages of mathematics," one of the boys grumbled, rolling his eyes in disgust. "You're a hard'un, Miss Pringle."

"I consider it part of my charm," she answered wryly, reaching out to tousle his hair. "No faces now, or I shall add an extra page of Latin to the tally."

Suddenly one of the children spotted Belle standing in the doorway and leapt to his feet. "Visitors!" he called, snapping to attention like a miniature soldier. The other children quickly followed suit, and even Miss Pringle rose, the book held in her arms as she dropped a curtsy.

"Good day, ma'am," she said, her cultured voice polite but wary. "I am Miss Pringle. May I help you?"

"Indeed you may, Miss Pringle," Belle said, smiling warmly. "I am Miss Portham, one of the guardians here, and if possible, I should like to have a word with you."

Miss Pringle raised her chin, but other than a slight tightening of her full lips, she revealed no sign of trepidation. "Certainly, Miss Portham," she answered calmly. "Only allow me to set the children to their tasks, and I shall join you in the front parlor."

Rather amused at the summary way she was being dismissed, Belle merely inclined her head, and began making her way toward the door. She paused en route to greet a few of the younger students, handing out smiles and candies with equal generosity. A few minutes later she was in the parlor, where Miss Pringle soon joined her. The other woman wasted no time in getting straight to the heart of the matter.

"I wasn't blackmailing the miserable creature," she said, her pointed chin jutting forward. "I was merely reminding him of his noble obligations. It's hardly *my* fault if he took it amiss."

Her reply was so like something Pip would say that Belle broke into a soft chuckle. "When one is forced to justify one's actions, Miss Pringle, one is acknowledging from the start that one is in the wrong," she said, with a warm smile. "However, if it will help ease your mind, I am not here to give you the boot."

Miss Pringle pushed her spectacles back on her nose and gave Belle a suspicious look. "You're not?"

"No. I can't say as I approve of your actions regarding Lord Perryvale, but I cannot fault your reasons for doing so. I am delighted you have taken such an interest in Amanda."

The scowl on the younger woman's face vanished as if by magic, and her thin face took on a luminous quality. "She is an angel," she said, dropping her distrustful air as she leaned forward in her chair. "One tries not to have favorites among the students, but with Amanda I could not help myself. There is something so very special about her . . ."

"I have noticed," Belle admitted, recalling her own affection for the solemn-eyed little girl. "She is a taking little thing."

"That is why I cannot understand that wretch—the duke's refusal to acknowledge Amanda," Miss Pringle said, hastily correcting herself. "What person in his right mind would want to deny kinship to such an adorable child?"

Memories of her own girlhood rose to torment Belle for a brief moment. "I cannot say, Miss Pringle," she replied with a sad smile, "but I do know one cannot force such a relationship upon another. If His Grace does not choose to acknowledge Amanda's existence, then we have no choice but to honor that decision. I trust I am making myself clear?"

Miss Pringle's light brown eyebrows met over her nose in a scowl. "No more letters?"

"Definitely no more letters," Belle said firmly. "From what Mrs. Langston has told me, your literary efforts have already caused quiet enough damage. Threats of suit for slander are not to be taken lightly, you know."

"I suppose not," Miss Pringle agreed with another scowl, "although I hardly think it can be considered slander when it is the truth."

Once more her resemblance to Pip brought a smile to Belle's face. She would have to take care the two never met, she decided whimsically, or heaven help the poor duke. "I have your word, then?" she asked, meeting the teacher's thoughtful gaze. "You won't pester His Grace with any more letters?"

Miss Pringle remained silent as she considered the matter. "Very well, Miss Portham," she said at last, setting her slender shoulders in a determined line. "I give you my most solemn vow that I shall never attempt to contact Lord Perryvale by post again."

It was only as Belle was returning home that the odd wording of Miss Pringle's promise occurred to her. Given the younger woman's rather forceful nature, she wondered if she should have demanded a more concise promise from her. If the girl was half so determined as Pip, she feared it was an oversight she would come to regret.

Nine

The family was enjoying a rare afternoon at home the following day when their tranquillity was disrupted by the arrival of Simon Dolitan, Julia's older brother. Upon hearing his deep voice in the hallway, Julia leapt to her feet, scattering her sewing as she rushed out to greet him.

"Simon!" she cried, throwing herself into his muscular arms. "Oh, I *knew* you would come!"

"Of course I came." He chuckled, giving her an affectionate hug. "What sort of man would I be to miss my own sister's ball, hm? Now, stand back so I can see what a fine lady you have become," he instructed, detaching her arms from about his neck and stepping back to admire her.

"Well, what do you think?" Julia demanded, tossing her golden curls with a girlish laugh. "Do I look like a countess?"

Simon's deep blue eyes grew even darker. "You look like a queen," he said, his voice husky. "Mama would have been very proud of you."

Belle watched the touching reunion from the door, feeling like an interloper. This is how it should be with families, she thought, blinking back tears. The love and support she'd always longed for and yet never had known. The thought made her feel more alone than ever.

Julia dragged Simon into the parlor, fussing over him until he laughingly threatened to return to the North, if only for some peace and quiet. Conversation became smoother after that, and Simon regaled them with tales of his journey and some investments he was considering.

"You might wish to look into that, Belle," he said, crossing one booted foot over another as he leaned back in his chair. "Low risks and good returns. It could make you a fortune."

"I already have a fortune," she reminded him with a chuckle. "But I promise to keep it in mind."

"Are you sure? For two thousand pounds you could realize three times that in less than five years time; sooner, if this steamboat I have been hearing so much about is a success."

"What on earth is a steamboat?" Georgiana demanded with a suspicious scowl. "It sounds a dreadfully vulgar thing to me."

"It is a boat propelled by steam rather than by wind or oar, ma'am," Simon explained good-naturedly. "It was invented by an American named Robert Fulton, and 'tis said it will revolutionize travel and commerce by the end of the decade."

"An American, hm?" Georgiana replied with a sniff. "Well, that would explain its vulgarity then."

Julia leapt into the silence that followed with an eager description of her new ball gown. Simon listened with every indication of interest, his expression grave as he offered his opinions when pressed. When that subject had been exhausted, she tentatively mentioned Toby, and a cold smile touched Simon's mouth.

"Ah yes, the young poet who has swept you off your feet," he said, his expression unreadable. "When am I to meet this paragon of masculine virtue?"

Belle choked on her mouthful of tea. Paragon of masculine virtue? *Toby?* It was all she could do not to laugh aloud, and she hastily composed her features.

"Now, Simon." Julia was regarding her brother with a chiding frown. "You know full well I said no such thing. I said he was all that I have ever wanted in a husband, and you know it."

"My mistake." He inclined his head. "But I would still like to know when I am to meet him . . . and his cousin. The earl of Colford, is he not?"

"Yes," Belle answered before Julia could speak. "He and I have known each other socially for a number of years, and I would be happy to vouchsafe for him. He is a most worthy gentleman."

Julia and Georgiana looked pleased and shocked by turns. Georgiana was the first to recover, her teacup held poised in her hand as she said, "Yes, the earl is quite a top-of-the-trees fellow, and Mr. Flanders is not without his charms. We are hoping you will agree to the match, as Julia seems quite determined to marry him."

"Are you, brat?" Simon turned to Julia.

"Quite determined, Simon," she said softly, her gaze meeting his. "With or without your permission."

He remained silent for a moment and then slowly nodded his head. "In that case, I had best meet the fellow. Cousin Belle? Do you think you might be able to arrange something?"

"Of course, Simon," Belle agreed, eager to help now that she knew Julia's heart was truly engaged. "I shall invite them for tea. Julia's ball is next week, and they are hoping to make their announcement then."

"We shall see," Simon said noncommittally. "We shall see. In the meantime let me tell you about another American invention I am thinking of investing in. It is called a cotton gin, and it will make cotton growing more profitable than ever ..."

Marcus was about to set out for the park with Lady Bingington when the footman arrived with the note from Miss Portham. He read it quickly, his expression darkening as he handed it back to the waiting servant.

"Is there an answer, my lord?" the young man asked anxiously. "The boy was told to wait for an answer."

"Have him tell Miss Portham that both Toby and I would be honored to meet Mr. Dolitan," he said, slapping his riding crop against the top of his Hessians. "Then I want you to go up and pry Mr. Flanders out of his study. Use force if you must, but I want him dressed and waiting when I return from my ride."

The footman broke into a wide grin. "Aye, my lord," he said. "I'll do that."

Marcus pulled his hat on and stalked outside, where a postboy was waiting with his stallion. After tossing the lad a shilling, he leapt up on the animal's back and began riding toward Hyde Park, where he had arranged to meet Lady Bingington and her stepson, Lord Wilbert. The ride had been set up last week, and he wondered if it meant the lovely widow was finally considering his suit.

Lord, he hated the necessity for this courting dance, he thought, his expression closed as he nodded to a few of his acquaintances who were already out enjoying the afternoon sun. He liked Charlotte well enough, and he respected her, but left to his own devices, he would never have thought of offering for her. Marriage had always been someplace in the hazy future for him, and when he envisioned his prospective bride, he'd always pictured her as younger, shyer, with golden hair and eyes . . .

He jerked in horror at the image, causing his horse to whinny in protest. He eased up on the reins at once, murmuring a quiet apology to the disgruntled animal. What the devil was the matter with him? he wondered, reaching up a shaking hand to brush the copper-colored hair out of his eyes. Belle was the one who had suffered the blow to the head, not him. So why was he the one to be suffering from delusions? And a delusion it was, to think Belle would consider marrying him, he told himself sternly. It was madness, and the sooner he put it from his mind, the better.

Lady Bingington and Lord Wilbert were waiting for him at their prearranged spot, and he doffed his hat with an easy smile. "Good afternoon, Lady Bingington, Lord Wilbert. I hope you are ready for a good gallop in the park. I need something to blow the cobwebs from my mind!"

"You and Mater may proceed ahead of me," Lord Wilbert said with an affected lisp, regarding Marcus through a pair of watery blue eyes. "I shall follow at a discreet distance. Mind you don't take any fences, Mama."

Lady Bingington exchanged a laughing glance with Marcus. "Yes, Hoppy, I shan't," she said, and then she and Marcus wheeled their mounts and went cantering across the grass.

"Hoppy?" Marcus asked once they were out of earshot.

"The nickname his brothers use when they wish to plague him," she said with a rich laugh. "He is next in line to the earldom of Hoppleigh, hence the diminutive form of address. He pretends to hate it, but I think he secretly likes the ridiculous name. He doubtlessly feels it has a certain je ne sais quoi."

"It has something, all right, if one doesn't mind being mistaken for a toad," Marcus agreed with a chuckle.

They rode along Rotten Row, exchanging greetings with friends and discussing a variety of topics. By the end of the ride he had decided to call upon her formally. Until now he'd been careful to avoid anything smacking of courtship, but now the time for caution was past. His debts were growing more pressing, and it was time he made his offer.

"I was wondering, Lady Bingington, if you were going to be at home tomorrow," he asked, his tone and manner formal.

"Yes, my lord, I am," she answered, making no attempt to hide her confusion. "May I ask why you wish to know?"

He drew a deep breath, realizing he was about to take the most important step of his life. If she agreed to his calling upon her, it would mean he was irrevocably committed to marrying her. If not, it would mean he was free . . .

"If you and your family will be at home, I thought to call upon you," he said, his gray eyes meeting hers. "I would like to speak to your stepsons."

There, he'd said it, he thought, his shoulders tensing as he waited for her answer. He could see by the expression on her face that she understood his unspoken meaning. Now all that remained was determining what she would do.

Lady Bingington remained silent, her lovely face giving away nothing of her most inner thoughts. She looked at Marcus for a long moment, and then slowly inclined her head. "Very well, my lord," she said, a note of quiet acceptance in her voice. "I would like that very much. Shall we say three o'clock?"

* * *

"Are you sure m'cravat is all right?" Toby demanded for the third time in as many minutes. "Don't know why I let that fool of a valet tie it in a Mathematical. The Oriental's all the rage now. Dolitan will take me for a quiz."

"He'll take you for a Bedlamite if you don't calm down," Marcus growled, fighting the urge to slap Toby's hands away from his cravat. He'd been plucking at it since they'd left the house, and it now hung in limp disarray about his fleshy throat. Hopefully Dolitan didn't care a fig about such things, he thought sourly, else he would refuse Toby on that basis alone.

"Don't think he'll quiz me, do you?" Toby demanded, abandoning his appearance for another worry. "Was never good at examinations, you know. Barely made it through Oxford."

"I know," Marcus replied, shuddering as he recalled the battle he'd waged to keep the dons from tossing out their indifferent pupil. "But don't worry, I much doubt Julia's brother will ask you to conjugate Latin verbs."

"I brought my poems with me," Toby said, patting the leather folio on his lap. "Thought he might be impressed. Most people are, you know, when they meet a *real* poet."

Marcus managed to answer without laughing, although it was a close thing. He was more afraid Mr. Dolitan would concern himself with Toby's financial situation, and then show them the door when he learned how desperate things really were. He knew most Cits would consider themselves lucky to be aligned to such an old and noble family as his, but from the little he'd learned of Simon Dolitan, he doubted a bankrupt title would hold much sway with him.

They arrived at Miss Portham's in less than

twenty minutes and were immediately ushered into the formal salon, where the family had gathered to receive them. After the introductions had been made, everyone took their seats, Toby sitting beside Julia, and Marcus beside Belle. Georgiana and Simon sat across from them, eyeing the two couples with varying degrees of interest. There was an uncomfortable silence before Belle took the lead.

"We were discussing America just before you arrived, my lord," she said, turning to give Marcus a tentative smile. "Simon is setting sail for Charleston at the end of June, and he has been telling us the most remarkable stories."

"Indeed?" Marcus inquired politely, eyeing the other man with veiled curiosity. Like his sister, Mr. Dolitan had wheat blond hair and sapphire blue eyes, but his harsh, remote features held no hint of Julia's gentle shyness. He looked every bit as hard and dangerous as he was reputed to be, and Marcus steeled himself for the coming confrontation.

"A fascinating country," Simon replied, returning Marcus's measuring stare. "I was there two years ago and have been anxious to return."

"Simon is going to invest in a steamboat!" Julia exclaimed with a nervous smile. "He says that soon all boats will be driven by steam. Didn't you, Simon?"

"Not all, imp." Simon's expression softened as he smiled at his younger sister. "But most of the ones engaged in commerce shall certainly be affected. That is why I am interested," he said in an aside to Toby and Marcus. "I own several mills in the North, and shipping my products to market has always been a problem. This could change everything."

The conversation became general after that, and

Belle allowed a quarter hour to pass until she set her cup to one side. "I am sure you gentlemen must have a great deal to discuss," she said, rising gracefully to her feet. "Come, Georgiana and Julia, we shall retire to the library."

Julia's lips trembled and for a moment it looked as if she might protest, but Toby reached out to take her hand. "You go with your cousins, my sweet," he said, giving her hand a paternal pat. "Men's business, don't you know. Don't worry, I shall be with you in a cat's whisker."

Once the ladies had taken their leave, Simon wasted little time in getting to the matter at hand. "So you intend marrying my sister, do you, Mr. Flanders?" he asked quietly, fixing Toby with an incisive look.

"I . . . yes, Mr. Dolitan, I do," Toby stammered, nervously licking his lips. "I adore her, and will do all that I can to see she never lacks for anything."

"And how do you intend doing that?" Simon asked coolly, his eyes never leaving Toby's face. "Other than a small annuity from your father's estate, you haven't a living to speak of."

Toby tugged on the collar of his cravat. "That's not precisely so, sir," he said, frantically wishing he were anywhere but here facing this cold-eyed devil. "I'm m'cousin's heir, you know, and stand to inherit an earldom. A fine estate and one of the oldest titles in England. Belle would be a countess, and—"

"I think Mr. Dolitan and I shall continue this conversation, Toby," Marcus interrupted, seeing the cold sneer forming on Mr. Dolitan's mouth. "As head of the family, it is my duty to discuss our finances with him. You may go."

Toby hesitated, torn between relief and the niggling suspicion that this was more his affair than Marcus's. "Are you certain, my lord?" he asked, his eyes flickering toward Mr. Dolitan. "Julia is my fiancée, and I still haven't explained about m'poems. I am published, you know," he said.

"So Julia has informed me." The cool note in Mr. Dolitan's voice made it obvious he was less than awed by this achievement.

"Oh." Toby rose to his feet and beat a hasty retreat, leaving Marcus and Simon to size each other up in silence.

"If you are half as clever as I have heard you are, then you already know Colford is in hock up to its rafters," Marcus said without preamble. "But you needn't think that has anything to do with Toby's offering for your sister. He genuinely loves her."

"I know that," Simon said, his opinion of the earl rising. "That is all that has kept me from forbidding the match outright. I'll not have my sister taken advantage of by anyone. Even," he added, smiling slightly, "by a published poet who may one day be an earl."

Some of the tension holding Marcus rigid relaxed at the other man's teasing words. "You will not oppose the marriage?"

"I should, for your cousin isn't at all the sort of man I would prefer for my sister," he said with surprising candor, his dark blue eyes meeting Marcus's. "Now, you, on the other hand, are far closer to what I had in mind when I first agreed to let Belle sponsor her. Don't suppose you'd care to cut your cousin out, would you?"

Marcus managed to hide his shock. "No, I would not," he said with alacrity. "Julia is as sweet as she is lovely, but she is almost young enough to be my daughter. I assure you my taste in brides does not run to children."

"That is reassuring," Simon drawled, wondering if the earl's tastes ran to older ladies . . . like his cousin. There had been something in his face when he'd greeted Belle that made him wonder, especially since Belle had the same expression in her eyes whenever she looked at him.

They spent the next half hour hammering out their financial differences before arriving at a marriage settlement acceptable to them both. Finally they were content, and as they rose to their feet, Simon offered Marcus his hand with a grin.

"It is probably just as well they don't allow gentlemen to sully their hands with trade, my lord," he said, his eyes dancing with amusement as he shook Marcus's hand. "I should hate to face a skilled negotiator like you in a matter of business. I have a feeling you'd make a dangerous opponent."

"Thank you, Mr. Dolitan," Marcus said, pleased by the compliment. "Coming from you, that is praise indeed."

Simon merely laughed, eyeing Marcus with a rueful expression. "Are you quite certain I can't convince you to marry Julia?"

"Quite certain, sir."

"Pity." Simon gave a regretful sigh. "You would have made a most interesting brother-in-law."

The news that Simon had agreed to the match was met with tears of joy from his sister, and relief from Toby. Belle decided the moment called for celebration, and ordered the butler to bring up a bottle of champagne from the wine cellar. Once the health of the happy couple had been toasted, talk turned to the ball. While Julia was describing her gown to Toby, Belle quietly drew Marcus to one side of the room.

"Thank you for your help, sir," she said, offering him a tentative smile as she studied his face. "I know you had more to do with Simon's agreeing to this marriage than did Toby, and I thank you. Julia would have been shattered had her brother opposed the match. They are very close, you know."

"So I gathered," Marcus drawled, his eyes flicking to the other side of the room where Mr. Dolitan was regarding his sister with an indulgent smile. "He is rather a formidable young man, and I should hate like the devil to cross him."

"Simon had it harder than Julia," Belle answered, thinking of the past several years. "He is related to my mother's side of the family, and although he was raised a gentleman, he's always worked for a living. He even spent a few years with the East India Company before returning to England to open his own mills. I know he's quite wealthy, and with our family connections, he'd be accepted into the *ton* without hesitation. Unfortunately he doesn't seem to have the slightest inclination to do so."

"Why?" Marcus asked.

"Because he is almost as stiff-necked as I am," Belle replied with a laugh. "He is proud of his accomplishments and sees no reason why he should pretend otherwise merely because 'gentlemen' aren't supposed to engage in trade."

"It does seem rather foolish," Marcus agreed slowly, although truth to tell, he'd never given the matter much thought. "Earning one's living with one's own hands can hardly be a less honorable profession than bleeding one's tenants dry the way many of our fine lords do."

The amazing observation had Belle choking on her wine, and she sent him an incredulous look. "Why, Lord Colford, never say there may be hope for you after all," she mocked, teasing him in a way she'd have considered impossible a few months ago. "I must write Pip a note at once, and

let her know we have a convert. Certainly no
proper Tory would ever utter such a thing!"

"Hellcat." Marcus reached out to flick a tanned
finger against her flushed cheek. "For your information, ma'am, Tories care equally for the plight
of the poor, even if we choose to go about show-
ing it in a different way. But enough of that now.
Is politics all you ever think of?"

"Perhaps," she murmured coyly, seeking refuge
in her wine and wondering what he would say if
he knew how many hours she'd spent brooding
over him and the disturbing feelings he stirred in
her.

Marcus watched her closely, curious what had
brought that pensive look to her face. In the weeks
since the start of the Season, he'd grown to know
her quite well, and he was learning just how
closely she guarded her emotions. Once, he'd have
dismissed that caution as mere coldness, but he
could see now that he was wrong. Belle was a
warm, loving woman, full of light and laughter,
and he was beginning to think of her far more
than was proper.

Because both families were attending the ball for
the Duke of Nottington's daughter, it was decided
they would travel together. Once the arrangements
were set, the other four adults withdrew to another room, discreetly allowing the engaged couple privacy to make their farewells. Georgiana also
said her good-byes, pleading a sudden headache
as she left Simon, Belle and Marcus alone in the
entryway.

"I was wondering if I might call upon you tomorrow, my lord," Simon said to Marcus. "I am
considering buying a mount, and I have it on great
authority that you are something of an expert in
regards to horseflesh."

Marcus hid his surprise at the graceful invitation. "I should be more than happy to assist you, sir," he said, his interest stirring. "Will you be going to Tattersall's?"

"Doesn't everyone?" Simon asked with a sardonic smile. "I've word of a two-year-old descended from the Godolphin Arabian, and I am interested in your opinion."

"Gray Boy?" Marcus had heard of the stallion, and had circumstances permitted, he would have been tempted to bid for the animal himself. "They say the bidding will open at ten thousand pounds."

The casual shrug Simon gave spoke for itself, and Marcus remained silent until a flushed but happy Toby arrived to join him. After the two men had departed, Julia drifted away, leaving Belle alone with Simon. "Ten thousand pounds?" she echoed incredulously. "For a horse?"

"For a thoroughbred," Simon corrected smoothly. "And it will probably cost closer to twenty thousand pounds before the bidding is done. Not that it matters; I intend to have the animal regardless of the price."

"Why?" Belle could scarce believe her ears. Despite his wealth, Simon had always been cautious with his money, and she couldn't believe he would wish to squander it so foolishly.

"I have my reasons," was all Simon would say, but the look in his eyes made Belle long to question him further. But now that they were finally alone, there was another matter she wished to discuss with him.

"Simon, would you come into my study, please?" she asked, gripping her hands together to hide their shaking.

"What is it?"

She drew a steadying breath. "It is rather pri-

vate," she said, her eyes not quite meeting his. "It
. . . it concerns the earl of Colford."

A slight smile touched Simon's hard mouth.
"Now, why doesn't that surprise me?" he drawled,
obviously amused. "Very well, Cousin. Lead on."

Ten

"Let me be certain I understand you," Simon said slowly, gazing at Belle as if she'd taken leave of her senses. "You want to buy up the earl's debts? All of them?"

"Only the most pressing ones," Belle clarified, still scarce believing what she was doing. She'd thought about it for days before coming to the conclusion it was the only way she could repay Marcus for the hurt she'd caused him. She'd considered having her solicitor or man of business handle the matter for her, but she decided she'd rather have Simon do it. Not only did she have faith in his business acumen, but she knew he could be trusted to hold his tongue. If there was any way this matter could be handled discreetly, Simon would know how to do it.

"I have already looked into the matter of his lordship's debts," Simon remarked dryly, his eyes still holding Belle's, "and believe me, they are all pressing. Especially the gaming debts his father left him."

"Then we shall start there," she said, trying to sound decisive. "It can be done . . . can't it?"

"To be sure. A man has but to pay the vowels, and sometimes a small incentive, and the debts are then his property. It is usually done to extract revenge, or place the other man in his power, but I suppose it could be done for altruistic reasons."

"You sound familiar with the process," Belle said, surprised at his detailed explanation. "Have you done this before?"

He gave her another enigmatic look. "I assume you don't want Colford to know the name of his benefactor?"

"Lord, no." Belle shuddered when she thought of Marcus's reaction. "Is that possible?"

Simon nodded. "I'll see to it at once, but first I want to know why you are doing this. If you're trying to curry his favor, I must warn you it won't work. From what I've observed of the earl, he has the devil's own pride, and I much doubt he'll appreciate your efforts."

The blunt observation made Belle's eyes frost with anger. "I am well aware of that, Simon," she said coolly, her chin coming up with pride. "Why do you think I wish to keep my involvement a secret? And I am most assuredly *not* attempting to curry his favor."

"Then why are you doing it?"

Belle glared at him, cursing herself for forgetting Simon's obstinate nature. She might have known he'd demand answers and then not rest until he had them. She considered spinning him a tale about wedding gifts and only wanting to help a family member, but it took only one look at his closed face to know that would never suit. It would have to be the truth then, she admitted glumly, and considered how much of the truth she could safely tell him.

"Less than a week ago I was kidnapped," she began. "I wasn't in any real danger as my assailants were nothing more than a trio of idiotic dandies on a lark, but I was knocked unconscious. The cubs panicked and brought me to Colford, who was able to bring me home without causing a scandal."

Other than a tightening of his jaw, Simon betrayed no emotion. "Why did they bring you to Colford? Was he involved?"

"No! One of the men was related . . . distantly . . . to the earl, and he didn't know where else to turn. I only thank heaven he had the presence of mind to act as he did, else I'm not sure what might have happened. They could have tossed me in the Thames." Her attempt at a joke was a poor one, if the look on Simon's face was any indication.

"Is that how you came by that knot on your head?" he asked, gesturing at the fading bruise on her forehead.

She raised a hand and gingerly fingered the discolored lump. "So much for my attempt to hide it," she said with a light laugh. "I was hoping no one would notice."

"I noticed." Simon's voice was soft. "What happened to these young dandies? Do you know their names?"

"No," she lied. "I never had a chance to see their faces. As for what happened to them, Lord Colford ordered them to leave London, and threatened them with a most unpleasant fate if they dared breathe a word of this to anyone. Satisfied?"

"No. He should have horse-whipped them first."

The soft violence in his deep voice made Belle blink in surprise. "Oh," was all she could think of to say. "Well, now that you know why I want to assist the earl, will you help me?"

"I've already said I would," he replied calmly. "In fact, I shall see to it at once. As I said, the gaming debts are by far the most pressing, so that is where I'll start." He rose to his feet, and started toward the door.

"Simon, wait."

"Yes?" He gave her a curious glance over his shoulder.

Belle moistened her lip. "You said you'd already looked into Marcus's debts," she said, choosing her words with care. "May I ask why?"

Simon's lips lifted in a cold smile. "Do you really think I'd allow Julia to marry without learning all that I could about her prospective groom?" he asked quietly. "I knew all that I needed to know about Mr. Flanders and his cousin within three days of receiving Julia's letter. Good-bye, Belle. I shall see you this evening."

The duke of Nottington's home was located a few short blocks from Belle's, but because of the heavy traffic clogging the streets, it took them almost half an hour to reach their destination. Simon kept his arms folded across his chest, glaring with obvious impatience at the long line of carriages pulled up in front of the elegant town house.

"We should have walked," he grumbled mutinously. "We'd already be inside by now."

"Idiot!" Georgiana gave him a none-too-gentle rap with her fan. "One does not *walk* to a ball; only think of the scandal it would cause!" She turned to Belle with an annoyed scowl. "Explain it to the boy!"

"He is only twigging you, ma'am," Marcus answered instead, exchanging a smile of commiseration with Dolitan. "But I must say he has the right of it; I've not seen the streets this crowded since the prince's soiree last year."

Georgiana muttered an annoyed reply beneath her breath, but said no more on the subject. Soon they were inside the stunning house, and after paying their respects to their hosts and their giggling daughter, they made their way into the ballroom, where an orchestra was playing. The strains of the waltz reached Marcus's ears, and he turned to Belle.

"Would you do me the honor, Miss Portham?" he asked, holding his arm out to her with an enticing smile. "Unless you have promised this dance to another man?"

"And if I have, sir?" she teased, her lips curving as she gazed up at him. He looked so handsome in his evening coat of midnight blue satin, his dark copper hair brushed to ruthless perfection, and her heart raced at the sight of him.

"Then I shall have to cut him out," he said, gathering her up in his arms and sweeping her out onto the dance floor. They completed two turns about the room before Belle was able to catch her breath.

"Neatly done, my lord," she applauded mockingly, one hand resting on his broad shoulder, while the other was cradled protectively in his warm grasp. "I can see where Toby gets his poetic nature; that was most dashing of you."

"Thank you, Miss Portham; I am delighted if my humble efforts have pleased you," Marcus replied, enjoying the feel of her in his arms. She moved as light as a breeze, easily matching her steps to his as they moved about the floor in time to the dreamy music. He'd waltzed with many ladies since coming to London, but for the first time he understood why Byron called it "the wanton waltz." He could feel her slender body brushing against his, and the tantalizing contact made him ache with the need for more.

Belle was equally affected by the feel of the muscular body so close to her own. She'd always found the waltz to be rather tiresome, suffering from either inept partners or annoying lechers who used the dance as an excuse to paw her.

Marcus, however, made of waltzing something magical, something dangerous that made her body burn with shameful longing.

"You are looking very beautiful this evening," Marcus said, his gray eyes gleaming with admiration as he studied her. "A new gown, is it not?"

"Yes, my lord, it is," she replied, feeling a rush of pleasure at his words. The aquamarine gown with its daring déclottage and tiny puff sleeves was the height of fashion, and quite unlike the coolly sophisticated gowns she usually wore. She told herself she'd purchased it because she was ready for a change of style, but she knew now that wasn't so. She'd bought the gown because she wanted Marcus to admire her.

"Marcus," he prompted.

"What?" The cryptic remark brought her eyes flashing to his face.

"Marcus," he repeated, and then smiled at her puzzled expression. "You promised to call me by my given name when we were alone," he reminded her, enjoying the play of emotions across her face. While they'd been dancing, he'd treated himself to the sheer pleasure of watching her, and he wondered now how he could have ever been so foolish as to think her cold. Her every thought and emotion was there on her face and in her amber-colored eyes; one merely had to know how to look for them.

Belle glanced ruefully about the crowded dance floor and then back at Marcus. "We are hardly alone now, sir," she chided, albeit with a tantalizing smile.

"Aren't we?" His arm tightened about her, his eyes holding hers in perfect intimacy. "I hadn't noticed."

The rules of propriety made a second dance unthinkable, and so Marcus had no choice but to return Belle to the corner where her older cousin was waiting. Nor was she alone. Lord Berwick was standing beside her, a smile of welcome on his face.

"Miss Portham, Lord Colford." He greeted them each with a polite bow before turning his attention on Belle. "I am delighted to see you have recovered from your accident, ma'am," he said, his hazel eyes sweeping over her as if searching for injury. "How are you feeling?"

"Other than being embarrassed at having caused such concern, I am fine, my lord," Belle replied, her earlier pleasure fading beneath her usual wariness. "Truly, other than a sore head, I was hardly hurt at all."

"That is reassuring." He'd availed himself of her hand and was carrying it to his lips. "I was terrified when I heard you'd been run down in the streets. Bad luck seems to be plaguing you of late, doesn't it?"

Belle knew he was referring to the incident with her coachman, Jackson, but the others had no such knowledge and demanded an explanation, which his lordship was more than happy to provide.

"Miss Portham's coachman left her stranded in a less-than-desirable section of London while he was enjoying a tipple," he said in an indulgent tone that set her teeth on edge. "Luckily I happened to be in the same area and was able to offer her the use of my coach. It was nothing." He shrugged his shoulders in a self-effacing manner that fooled no one, least of all the man who stood watching him with eyes of frost.

"Do you often frequent less-than-desirable sections of London, my lord?" Marcus asked coolly, his fingers curling in fists at the sight of the other man holding Belle's hand. It touched something hard and dangerous deep inside of him, and it was all he could do not to smash the fatuous look from his face.

"Eh?" Berwick looked confused for a moment. "Oh, that, er . . . no. I was returning from visiting an old friend when I saw Miss Portham standing in front of her school. A fortuitous accident, you might say."

"I might say that, yes."

The clipped reply caused an uneasy pause, and Marcus muttered a polite excuse, beating a hasty retreat before he embarrassed himself beyond any hope of redemption. Lady Bingington had also been invited, but there was no sign of her, and he concluded she must have attended another party. He spent the next hour wandering about the crowded rooms, speaking casually to his friends and doing his best not to look for Belle.

He knew she'd danced with Berwick, curse his black soul, but after that, she'd remained on the side, chatting with the small circle of intellectual females who were her friends. At one point she must have sensed his eyes on her, because she glanced up, and for one glorious moment their eyes met and held in perfect communion. It lasted less than a second, but the impact left him reeling. He was still trying to come to terms with its power when he felt a presence beside him. He turned and found Lord St. Ives had joined him.

"She is lovely, is she not?" Alex asked calmly, raising his glass of champagne to his lips. "The first time I saw her, I thought her quite the most exquisite creature I'd ever seen."

"She's beautiful," Marcus corrected, his eyes drifting back to where Belle had been joined by another of her many friends.

"But cold," Alex added, flicking Marcus a speculative look. "I recall the time Kingsford told me

I'd get more warmth from one of the Elgin Marbles."

"Kingsford is an ass."

"You'll get no argument from me, but what about you? You're the one who first called her The Golden Icicle."

Marcus's cheeks turned a dull red. "I am also an ass," he muttered, feeling the familiar shame washing over him. "Someone should have taken me out and beat the living devil out of me."

"It sounds as if someone already has," Alex observed wryly. "How did it go this afternoon? I just met Miss Dolitan's intimidating brother, and I must say I was impressed. If he ever decides to stand for a seat, I'd be more than happy to sponsor him. I believe in backing winners."

"As do I." Marcus was pleased Alex shared his opinion of Simon. "And fortunately for all, everything went splendidly. Toby and Miss Dolitan will be formally announcing their engagement at her ball."

"Congratulations." Alex raised his glass in a mock salute. "This must take some of the pressure from you, hm?"

"What do you mean?" Marcus turned to his friend with a frown.

"I know how hard you've been working to save your estates," Alex said simply. "A generous marriage portion will doubtlessly go a long way toward shoring up your fortune."

Marcus's lips thinned at his friend's words. As much as he would have liked to deny Alex's observation, it was the truth, and that only added to the bitter frustration eating at him. "We were able to come to terms," he said stiffly, his eyes not meeting Alex's. "A portion of the settlement will go to the general management of my estate, but only until such time as I marry and produce a son.

Once Toby is no longer considered my heir, the payments stop."

"A rather poor incentive to force a man to the altar," Alex observed with a chuckle. "Speaking of which, how goes your courtship of the widow? Will you be offering for her soon?"

Marcus glanced back at Alex, his eyes narrowing with suspicion. "You seem damned interested in my personal life all of the sudden," he said, scowling. "What the devil is going on?

"You may blame Phillipa," Alex answered with a laugh. "She has been quizzing me about you a dozen times a day since we returned from the country. Lucky for you, I'm not the jealous sort, else you would find yourself naming your seconds."

"Why should the viscountess be so interested in me?" Marcus asked, wondering if perhaps she was asking for Belle's benefit.

"God knows. I may love her to distraction, but I gave up attempting to fathom her mind long ago. Although it could be because she has a prospective bride in mind for you should Lady Bingington fail to come up to scratch. She has been mentioning a certain Lilian Petrie almost as often as she has been mentioning you; an ominous development, I am sure you will agree."

"Lilian Petrie?" The name was not familiar to Marcus.

"The daughter of one of my late neighbors," Alex explained. "He was a world traveler, and died of some mysterious fever while returning from his latest journey. His death left his daughter well heeled, and now Pip has it in her mind to bring her to London."

"Indeed?" Marcus was only half listening. Belle had been joined by Lord Berwick, and they appeared to be having an animated conversation.

"Yes, but I wouldn't lick my lips in eager anticipation if I were you. The lady has become a fast friend of my wife's, and you must know that means she is a bluestocking."

Marcus managed to tear his gaze away from Belle long enough to give the viscount a puzzled look. "Why should that matter?"

"That desperate, are you?" Alex shook his head. "I'd best not tell Pip, else she'll send for Lilian on the next coach."

"No," Marcus corrected, "I meant why do you think it should matter to me whether or not a lady is an intellectual? I've no use for empty-headed females."

"I thought you despised the race," Alex said, defending himself with wide-eyed innocence. "I seem to recall your making any number of pithy remarks when I was courting Phillipa. What else was I to think? Oh, and I should also warn you my beloved wife has been polluting Miss Petrie with her political radicalism. The last thing she gave her before we left was a rather well-thumbed copy of *A Vindication of the Rights of Women.*"

"Where is your wife?" Marcus asked, deciding to ignore the provocation of that last remark. "I haven't seen her."

"She wasn't feeling well, but she insisted I come without her," Alex said, an odd glow turning his eyes to purest blue. "You may be the first to know, Marcus. I will be a father by year's end."

"Alex!" Marcus turned to his friend with delight. "That is wonderful! My congratulations!" And he extended his hand to Alex, clapping him heartily on the shoulder.

"We're pleased," Alex admitted, still dazed with happiness. "I only wish the minx might have told me sooner. I'd never have exposed her to the London air if I'd known."

"Why didn't she?" Marcus was curious. "I hadn't thought your wife was so interested in society."

"She's not, but you must be mad if you think she'd allow me to miss a single session of Parliament. I've married a harsh taskmistress, Colford, and she is determined to keep my nose to the grindstone."

The foolish grin on his face indicated he obviously considered this no great hardship, and Marcus was about to tease him about that fact when he added, "I thank God their original scheme failed and I didn't find myself shackled to Miss Portham. I shudder to think what my fate might have been then, for I doubt she'd settle for her husband reaching anything less than a minister post."

"*What?*"

Alex closed his eyes, uttering a word he'd learned from one of his top sergeants. "Damn," he said, opening his eyes and shooting Marcus a guilty look. "Upon your life, you must never utter a word of this to anyone. Phillipa would have my head if she knew I'd broken her confidence."

"Of course you may rely on my discretion," Marcus promised, shaken by the image of his friend and Belle married.

"Precisely what I said to Pip," Alex grumbled, and then leaned closer. "Do you recall last year when I got involved in that bloody wager to escort Pip to Prinny's ball?"

"How can I forget? The whole damned thing was Toby's fault!"

"Don't remind me. At any rate, what I did not know until much later was that Pip and Miss Portham also had a wager of their own ... a wager involving me."

Marcus wasn't sure he cared for the direction of

the conversation. "What did the wager involve?" he asked.

"It involved Miss Portham marrying me so that she could become my political hostess."

"The devil you say!" Marcus exclaimed in outrage.

"It makes a certain sort of sense when you think of it," Alex replied calmly, his eyes resting on Miss Portham. "By marrying me, she would gain the access to the political power she desires. And there is no denying that she would make the perfect wife for such a politician: beautiful, poised, and of course, her fortune wouldn't go amiss, either. Certainly Berwick seems to think so," he added with a cynical laugh.

Marcus stood as if turned to stone, his jaw clenching as he watched Belle and the marquess. "She can't seriously be considering him," he said, his voice harsh even to his own ears.

"No, but I would say it is obvious he is considering her," Alex answered with a shrug. "And why not? It sounds a perfect base for a marriage to me: her gold for his power."

"It sounds as cold-blooded as hell!" Marcus exclaimed, horrified by the viscount's cool observation.

"And your courting of Lady Bingington is any different? Her money for your title?" Alex demanded, them grimaced with regret. "I'm sorry, Marcus, I should never have said that."

Marcus gave a bitter laugh. "Why not?" he asked, turning bleak eyes on his friend. "It is the truth."

"You are trying to save your inheritance, blast it! There's not a man here who would fault you for what you are doing!"

"No?" A terrible pain filled Marcus as he

watched Belle and Lord Berwick leave. "Perhaps I blame myself."

"A babe? Oh, Pip, how wonderful!" Belle exclaimed, her eyes misting with tears as she enveloped the other woman in an exuberant hug. "I am so happy for you!"

"I can tell," Pip replied sardonically, although she returned Bell's embrace with equal enthusiasm. "And with that in mind, I have a favor I should like to ask of you."

"Anything," Belle promised, dabbing at her eyes as she returned to her seat. It was the afternoon following the ball at the Nottingtons', and Belle had called upon her friend to make sure she was well. They were sitting in Pip's elegant study, and the sun streaming through the mullioned windows filled the room with soft, golden light.

"I want you to stand as godmother."

Belle paled, her throat tightening painfully. "Godmother?"

Pip's green eyes were suspiciously bright as she took Belle's hand in hers. "You are my dearest friend in the world," she said softly. "Who else would I wish to act as my child's godmother?"

At first Belle couldn't speak, emotion making it impossible to form a coherent sentence. Finally she found her voice. "I would be honored," she said, the words not quite steady.

"Good, I am glad that is settled," Pip said, wiping furiously at the tears streaming down her cheeks. "I *hate* this! I seem to dissolve into a watering pot without the slightest provocation these days, but Aunt assures me 'tis only to be expected, given my condition."

"I understand," Belle replied gently, aware of an aching, hollow feeling deep inside her. She'd never given children much thought, but now the very

notion was enough to bring a fresh spurt of tears
to her eyes. She was more than a quarter of a century old, and she wondered if she would ever
know what it felt like to hold her babe in her
arms.

Pip saw the wistful pain in Belle's eyes and
quickly changed the conversation to another topic.
"Where is Julia?" she asked brightly. "Is she
spending the day with her brother?"

"No, she and Georgiana are calling upon some
old friends," Belle said, grateful for Pip's tact. "As
for Simon, he is spending the afternoon with Lord
Colford looking at some overpriced piece of horseflesh. Only imagine spending ten thousand
pounds for one animal ... Men!"

"Ah, you must be talking about Gray Boy," Pip
said with a wise nod. "Alex speaks his name with
the reverence one usually reserves for royalty, but
fortunately he hasn't shown any serious interest in
either breeding or racing the wretched creatures
... thank heavens."

They continued discussing masculine foibles
while the maids bustled about them preparing a
sumptuous tea. When they were alone once more,
Pip turned the conversation back to Simon.

"If your cousin is spending the afternoon with
Colford, I gather that you and he have made your
peace," she observed, studying Belle over the rim
of her cup. "You can actually say his name without throwing something."

Belle busied herself with her tea, unable to meet
Pip's eyes. "I've never thrown anything in my
life," she muttered, her cheeks coloring with embarrassment.

"No, but you certainly looked as if you'd like
to," Pip answered with a mischievous laugh. "But
don't equivocate. Have the two of you settled
your differences?"

Belle was uncertain how to answer. In many ways she and Marcus had grown shockingly close, yet in others they were further apart than when they were the bitterest of enemies. She tried to find the words to explain this dichotomy, but none would come. Her feelings for Marcus were a Gordian knot of confusion, and she was beginning to fear she would never unravel them. "Yes," she said at last, "we have settled our differences."

Pip gave her a considering look, a smile of delight playing about her lips. "Good," she said in satisfied tones. "That is what I thought."

His conversation with Alex was uppermost in Marcus's mind as he presented himself at Lady Bingington's home on Hanover Square the following afternoon. He'd spent most of last night wrestling with his conscience and his pride, but he was no closer to resolving his dilemma. The only thing he had concluded was that regardless of the consequences, he would be completely honest with Charlotte. He would not offer her marriage under the guise of undying love. If she accepted, fine. If not . . .

"I am so sorry to keep you waiting," Lady Bingington apologized as she breezed into the parlor where Marcus had been cooling his heels. "But Bertie—he is my grandson—is staying with us, and nothing would do but his grandmama feed him his luncheon. I trust you haven't been waiting long?'

"Not long at all," Marcus assured her, carrying her hand to his lips. "Although I must say it sounds rather odd to hear one so young and lovely as you speak of grandchildren. You look scarce beyond childhood yourself."

"False flattery, sir, but after the morning I have had, I thank you," Charlotte said, her eyes bright with laughter. "But pray, will you not be seated? The duke and the others will be joining us shortly."

Marcus remained standing, feeling as if he were about to leap into a bottomless void. This was the moment he had been waiting for, the moment upon which his entire past and present rested, and now that it had arrived, he wondered what the devil he was going to do. Drawing a deep breath to steady his nerves, he met the duchess's candid gaze.

"I suppose you know why I have come," he said, his quiet voice giving no hint of his inner turmoil.

"I have a fair idea," Charlotte responded dryly, her lips curving in a slight smile. "You wish to marry me."

"Yes, that is correct," he replied, startled by her blunt reply. "Do you know why?"

"To salvage your estates, I should imagine."

Again her straightforward response left him feeling decidedly rattled. "And you do not mind?" he asked, trying to envision how Belle would have reacted to such a bloodless proposal.

Lady Bingington gave a cool laugh. "I am one and thirty, my lord; I lost my girlish illusions long ago. I know full well that people of our class seldom marry for something so self-indulgent as love. It is the way of our world, and I much doubt it will ever change."

"Then . . . you accept my suit?" Marcus pressed, his heart racing with fear. What he did not know was whether it was racing from fear she would reject him, or fear she would say yes.

"I didn't say that."

"I beg your pardon?" He frowned at her reply.

Charlotte rose from her chair and walked over to stand before Marcus, her expression serious as she gazed up at him. "I was eighteen when my parents told me I was to marry the duke," she said simply. "At the time I did as they asked, knowing it was my duty and that I really had no other choice. I won't pretend I was happy in my marriage, but I was . . . content, I suppose is the word. I did my best to be a good wife to George, and I like to think I made his final years happy ones.

"Since my husband's death, I have tried to be a good dowager; supportive of my grown stepsons, yet not demanding too much from either them or the estate. I am now learning to be a good grandmother to the children's children, and much as I enjoy the role, I have come to the realization that I want more."

"What more do you wish?" he asked, following her thoughtful explanation with intense concentration. "Children of your own?"

"Perhaps, but more importantly, I want something of my own, something for myself. Does that sound hopelessly selfish to you?" She sent him an anxious look.

"No," he denied, shaking his head. "It doesn't."

"I have thought about this a great deal," Charlotte said painfully, "and I have decided that to marry again, merely for duty or because it is expected of me, would be a folly." She raised her dark eyes to his. "My lord, may I ask you something?"

"Of course," he said, anticipating what her question would be.

"Do you love me?"

Now that the moment had arrived, he knew he could not lie. She deserved more than deceit, more than the half of a heart which was all he could offer her. The rest of his heart belonged to Belle. He loved her. Once he admitted that, the tangle of his emotions suddenly unraveled, and he wondered how he could have been so blind.

The truth of his love overwhelmed him, filling him with the wildest exaltation and the deepest despair. He wanted to shout it to the heavens, to whisper it to Belle in the sweetest of intimacies. But first he had to deal with Charlotte. He opened his eyes and met her steady gaze.

"No, my lady," he said softly, his expression filled with tender regret. "I do not."

"Do you love another?"

Belle's face filled his mind, and he gave a sad smile. "Yes," he admitted, savoring the sweetness of the words, "I do."

Charlotte hesitated, then offered him her hand. "Then I think it best that we not say another word," she said with gentle understanding. "I will tell my stepsons you were unable to wait. I am sure they will understand. And, my lord?"

"Yes?"

She stood on tiptoe and pressed a kiss to his cheek. "Good luck."

Eleven

Simon was waiting when Marcus returned home, and after pausing only long enough to change out of his formal clothing, they were on their way to Tattersall's. Much to Marcus's relief, the younger man seemed as disinclined to idle conversation as was he, and they passed most of the short journey in companionable silence.

They were just approaching the exclusive establishment when he said, "How is your sister this morning, Mr. Dolitan? I recall Toby mentioning she and Mrs. Larksdale were calling upon some friends. He seemed cast down at the thought he'd not be able to see her until this evening."

"You should have seen Julia," Simon replied sardonically, his lips curving at the memory. "She sighed and moped about like a character out of a second-rate drama until Belle threatened to have her purged. She brightened considerably after that."

"I can imagine," Marcus replied, and then cleared his throat. "And Miss Portham? How is she? Last night's exertions didn't prove too much for her after her unfortunate accident?"

"She is fine," Simon assured him, his blue eyes enigmatic as he studied the other man. "Belle told me about the kidnapping," he said bluntly, "and I want the names of those men involved. No one touches a member of my family and escapes unscathed."

The icy menace in his deep voice made Marcus look at him with renewed respect. "They didn't escape unscathed," he said calmly, fixing him with a cool look. "I have seen to that."

"Perhaps, but Belle is *my* cousin, and therefore my responsibility. If you won't tell me what I wish to know, I will simply find out on my own."

Although Marcus could understand his need for vengeance, he couldn't allow Dolitan to ferret out the truth. Not just for Toby's sake, he realized, but for Belle's as well. She had suffered enough, and he was determined to protect her as best he could. "The matter has been resolved, Dolitan," he said, his voice every bit as cold as Simon's. "Quietly and without a breath of scandal. If you go poking into matters now, that could well change, and it will be Belle who pays the price. What is more important to you—your cousin or your need for revenge?"

Simon glared at him, and then heaved a heavy sigh. "You are a hard bastard, Colford," he said, his expression sulky. "And curse it, you are right. Not that I intend letting the matter drop altogether," he added, shooting him a warning look. "One of these days I shall have the truth, and when I do, I'll take my revenge in such a way that Belle won't be touched."

Marcus gave him a respectful look that was slightly tinged with curiosity. "It sounds as if the anger that provokes revenge is a familiar emotion to you," he observed quietly. "But a man needs more than vengeance to live, you know."

A glacial sheen turned Simon's eyes to blue ice. "You are wrong, my lord," he said, his tone lacking all inflection. "Sometimes revenge is the only reason to live."

Marcus digested the other man's cold observation in silence. He sensed there was far more to the story than those cryptic words indicated, and for a moment he considered offering Simon his counsel. In the next moment, however, he was rejecting the altruistic impulse. Not only did he suspect such an offer would be firmly spurned, but he'd have felt like a damned hypocrite offering any advice. Only look at the tangle he had made of his own life, he thought bitterly, and then turned his head to gaze out the window.

They spent the rest of the day at the Turf Club, examining horses and enjoying each other's company in the quiet way men have. Their odd conversation was never alluded to again, not even when Simon paid fifteen thousand pounds for the colt they had come to see. The other man bidding on the horse seemed to take his loss as a personal affront, but Simon accepted it coolly in stride.

While they walked about admiring the horses, Marcus's mind kept going back to his meeting with Lady Bingington. Now that she'd put an end to his hopes for a *mariage de convenance*, he knew he should begin looking about for another prospect, but he did not see how that could be possible. Now that he'd admitted he loved Belle, the thought of marrying another woman was profoundly distasteful. He wondered if he would be able to do it, even if by failing to do so, he could lose his estate.

God, what a tangle, he thought, his face expressionless as he listened to Simon's occasional remarks. Once, Colford had been all the world to him, all the cared about, but now there was Belle. If he could have her, he would sacrifice his estate without another thought, but the bitter truth was that he would lose both. He wasn't so foolish as to think she would consider his suit for a single moment. Like Lady Bingington, he'd lost his illusions long ago, and he doubted Belle would be willing to offer her fortune and her hand to a penniless lord. Perhaps if she loved him, it would be different, but as she did not . . .

On the return journey to Marcus's house, Simon decided he'd had enough of the earl's brooding silence. Folding his arms across his chest, he leaned back against the squabs of his hired coach and fixed Marcus with a thoughtful look. "It seems to me that Julia isn't the only one who stands in need of a purging," he remarked with a half smile. "You have been quiet as the grave, my lord, and much as I appreciate a man who knows how to hold his tongue, I am growing weary of my own voice. Is something amiss?"

Marcus stirred restlessly, his eyes flickering toward Simon's sardonic face. "I beg your pardon, Dolitan," he said, forcing his bleak thoughts to one side. "I am afraid I have a great deal on my mind. My apologies for being such poor company."

"Not at all," Simon answered, for having seen the extent of the burden Colfold had inherited, he could well understand his pensive mood. The only wonder was that he'd managed to keep the estate out of bankruptcy before now, and the fact that he had said a great deal about both his tenacity and his business abilities. As a man who admired such things, Simon determined to do what he could to assist him.

"Your knowledge of horses is amazing, my lord," he said, pretending to study the traffic flowing past the coach. "Have you ever given thought to investing in a farm? You would do rather well, I think."

Marcus gave a bleak laugh. "Thank you,

Dolitan, but I fear an investment of any kind is above my touch at the moment."

Simon paused, knowing he had to tread a fine line if he hoped to succeed. "An investment need not always be monetary in nature, my lord," he said, striving for indifference. "Experience is sometimes a far more important commodity."

"What do you mean?" Marcus asked, intrigued despite his dark thoughts.

"I have more than enough to invest in my own stud farm," he said, deciding the time had come to lay his cards upon the table. "But I scarce know one end of a horse from another. This gives me one of two unattractive alternatives. I can either attempt to run the thing myself, or I can place myself in the hands of a manager and pray he doesn't fleece me in the bargain. Neither of these choices appeals to me, as I am sure you can understand."

Marcus didn't pretend not to understand precisely. "Are you attempting to hire me as your steward, Mr. Dolitan?" he asked, his jaw clenching with suppressed fury.

"Not at all," Simon replied, equally cool. "I want you to be my partner in a thoroughbred farm. I will provide the horses, you provide the knowledge and the proper business connections to the *ton*. What say you, your lordship? Have we a deal?"

The next two days were too filled with activity for Belle to have much time for brooding. Although Julia's betrothal had yet to be announced, word had somehow leaked out, and invitations for the young couple arrived with each morning's post. Ideally Julia should have handled matters herself, but she'd become so dreamy-eyed of late, she was no earthly good, and Belle finally admitted defeat and resumed the task. She was leafing through a fresh pile of invitations one morning when Gibson announced Lord Berwick had called and was waiting upon her in the drawing room.

For a moment she considered having the butler tell him she was indisposed, but she reluctantly decided that was hardly the proper way to treat a marquess. Instructing Gibson to inform his lordship that she would join him in a few minutes, she dashed upstairs to tell Georgiana of their caller, and then hurried into her rooms to change into a more attractive gown.

Georgiana was pressing cakes and tea upon the marquess when she made her appearance, a hand held out in greeting as she approached him. "Good afternoon, my lord," she said with a smile of polite welcome pinned to her lips. "What a pleasant surprise to find you here! I trust you are well?"

"Quite well, Miss Portham," he answered, his eyes warm as he carried her hand to his lips for a brief kiss. "I realize I ought to have written first, but as I was nearby, I decided to take the risk of calling unannounced. I hope I haven't come at an inopportune time?"

"Of course not, my lord!" Georgiana fairly beamed at him. "We were just sitting about wishing for company, weren't we, my dear?" And she turned a commanding gaze on Belle.

"Pining for it," she replied dutifully, wondering what new maggot was gnawing at her cousin's brain.

"There, you see?" Georgiana said to Berwick with a fatuous smile. "You are more than welcome for a comfortable chat. Although I hope you will excuse me if I sit over by the fire; these old bones, you know, and it's been so horribly damp of late, I quite ache all over."

She hurried over to the far side of the room with

an agility that made her claim for frailty patently false. Belle gave her visitor a faintly apologetic smile. "Subtlety has never been Georgiana's long suit," she said, indicating with a wave of her hand that he should resume his seat. "I hope you don't mind, for she means well."

"Not at all, Miss Portham," he said, leaning toward her with a conspiratorial smile. "In fact, I appreciate her tact as this will give me a moment to be private with you."

"Oh?" Belle wasn't certain she cared for the sound of that.

"Pray, don't be offended," he said hastily, hearing the displeasure in her voice. "My intentions are strictly honorable, I assure you."

Belle liked the sound of that even less, and gave him a haughty look. "I would ask that you say no more, my lord," she said, drawing on her reputation for coldness. "I am pleased that you have called, but that is all."

"Of course, I understand completely," he said, patting her hand as if she were a child. "This is neither the time nor the place, but I can wait until we're alone ... truly alone, before saying more. Mum's the word."

"Lord Berwick, I fear you have misunderstood me. I meant—"

The door opened without warning, and Julia came waltzing in on Toby's arm. Simon and Marcus brought up the rear, and at the sight of the visitor, both men stopped short. Marcus's eyes narrowed in possessive fury to see the other man sitting so intimately with Belle, and he moved forward without thinking.

"Ah, this is where you are, my lord," he drawled, his voice stopping just short of insolence. "We missed you in the debating sessions this morning."

"I had other matters on my mind, Colford," the marquess answered loftily. "Politics isn't everything, you know."

"Perhaps, but I wouldn't admit as much in front of Miss Portham. She is of the opinion that politics is the raison d'être of any honorable man; is that not so, ma'am?" His gray eyes cut to Belle's face.

Although she couldn't recall ever saying as much to him, it was close enough to the truth to suit Belle. "And not just gentlemen, my lord," she added with a proud toss of her head. "We ladies are not totally disinterested in such matters."

"Of course you aren't, Miss Portham," Berwick said, giving her hand another pat. "And such interest is most becoming."

If the idiot touched her one more time, he would strangle him with his own cravat, Marcus decided savagely, his hands balling into fists. He remembered what Alex had said about their making a suitable match, and it sent a shaft of agony through him. He could bear anything but for her to enter into such a bloodless arrangement.

If Berwick patted her hand like an indulgent papa one more time, she would dump the teapot over his head, scandal or nay, Belle thought, her patience evaporating. It didn't help her lacerated nerves that Marcus was glaring down at them like an outraged husband, and she would feel her head beginning to pound from the tension. Wonderful, she thought glumly, a migraine was all she needed to make this day a complete disaster.

To her surprise, Julia hurried forward, her golden eyebrows gathered in a frown as she studied her. "Why, Belle, you are positively white!" she chided, brushing past Marcus to kneel at her side. "You're getting one of your headaches, aren't you?"

"I am afraid that I am," Belle said, grasping at

Julia's concern with desperate gratitude. She knew it was cowardly to quit the field, but she was simply too weary to care. There were undercurrents in the room she didn't understand, and she needed to be alone so that she could sort them out. She turned to the marquess since he was closest to her.

"I hope you will pardon me, sir, but I am afraid I must cry off," she said with a tight smile. "Thank you for stopping by."

"Of course, of course." He was all gallantry. "My dearest mother was a slave to the vapors; I quite understand. May I call upon you tomorrow and take you for a drive in the park?"

"That will be fine, sir," Belle promised, although she had no intention of getting into a carriage with him. She'd send him a note tomorrow pleading illness, she decided, murmuring excuses to the others as she took her leave.

To her surprise, Julia insisted upon accompanying her up to her room, gently assisting her into a wrapper and into bed. "And mind you stay there," she scolded, brushing a lock of hair from Belle's forehead. "I don't want you to stir so much as an inch until after tea!"

"Yes, Julia," Belle said, too exhausted to be other than faintly amused at the younger woman's peremptory manner. She lay on the bed with her eyes closed, listening as Julia bustled about the room closing drapes and whispering instructions to Annette. Finally she was alone and she snuggled down against the pillows, surrendering gratefully to the comforting darkness.

"I still say you ought to have sent for a physician," Marcus said, his mouth tight with disapproval as he glared at the closed door of the drawing room. "What if her head injury is plaguing her? She could fall asleep, and never wake up."

"I think there is little danger of that," Simon replied soothingly, wryly intrigued by the earl's anger. "I've known my cousin several years, and she has had these headaches before. It will pass if she is left alone."

Marcus sent him a black scowl, annoyed by his indifference to his cousin's pain. When he'd seen her white face and the suffering that dulled her golden eyes, it had taken all of his control not to sweep her into his arms and carry her off to his house, where she could receive proper care. It was evident no one here gave a fig about Belle, he decided righteously, turning his icy gaze on Mrs. Larksdale, who was enjoying her tea with seeming unconcern.

"And what of you, ma'am?' he demanded haughtily. "Aren't you at least going to go up and check on your cousin's welfare?"

"Why would I do that?" Georgiana asked. "The poor dear is exhausted, and the last thing she needs when she has one of these attacks is a lot of people hovering over her. Rest and complete silence, that is the cure that will prove the most effective."

Marcus said nothing, accepting sullenly that there was little he could do about the situation. He would call upon her tomorrow, he promised himself, forcing his tense muscles to relax. If he found she was still unwell, he would fetch the doctor himself, and the devil with the proprieties!

After several abortive attempts to drag Toby away from Julia, Marcus gave up and returned home alone. There was a note from his solicitor waiting for him, and after reading the urgently worded missive, he set out for Harley Street, his expression resigned. Since notifying the other man of his failure to make a prosperous marriage, he'd been expecting such a letter, and he wondered how bad the news would be. Less than fifteen minutes after walking into Mr. Hampson's rooms, however, is grim expression had changed to one of incredulity.

"What do you mean my debts have been bought up?" he demanded, struggling to understand what he was hearing. "How could such a thing happen without my permission?"

"Quite easily, actually," the solicitor explained with a bright smile. "One has but to pay your creditors the amount owed them, and your vowels become their property. It is done all the time and is, I assure you, quite legal."

Marcus ran a hand through his hair, fighting a mixture of emotions, from relief to angry suspicion. Just what the devil was going on? he wondered. And how would it impact the estate? He fixed the other man with a narrow-eyed look. "Does this mean I am now free of debt?"

"Unfortunately not," Mr. Hampson replied with a regretful sigh. "It merely means that rather than owing the sum to one party, you now owe it to another."

"Who?"

The solicitor shuffled his papers and nervously cleared his throat. "I . . . That is the difficulty, my lord," he admitted, avoiding Marcus's eyes. "The party . . . whoever he is, has chosen to remain anonymous."

Simon's hard face flashed into Marcus's mind. He wondered if the other man had paid off his debts for some Machiavellian purpose known only to him, or if some unknown enemy had purchased them in order to drive him onto the rocks. "Is there a way I can find out?" he asked, fighting to keep his voice level.

"Anything is possible, I suppose," Hampson replied after a thoughtful pause. "Although I don't see why you should bother. Your new creditor has made it obvious he doesn't intend pressing for immediate payment, and has even hinted at a willingness to overlook several of the older debts."

"How generous of him," Marcus drawled, his lips curling in an unpleasant smile. "But what happens if he changes his mind and demands immediate payment? What then?"

Again the solicitor would not meet his eyes. "Then I suppose things could become rather difficult," he admitted awkwardly, "but I don't think—"

"No, I can see that you do not," Marcus interrupted, surging impatiently to his feet. "Perhaps you are willing to put your faith in this mysterious benefactor, but I cannot afford to be so naive," he said in his coldest voice. "Whoever he is, he holds the fate of Colford in his hands, and I would know his name. Do you understand me, Hampson?"

"I . . ." Hampson started to protest, and then swallowed his words at the deadly look on the earl's face. "Yes, my lord," he concluded. "I understand perfectly."

Belle awoke the next morning to find her headache quite gone. While she was grateful to be free of the pain, she couldn't help but feel a twinge of regret. A headache would have provided the perfect excuse to avoid Berwick's rather persistent company, and now she would have to think of something else. For a brief moment she considered feigning a return of her illness, but she dismissed that as being beneath her. She'd never resorted to such tiresome feminine ploys before, and she wasn't about to start doing so now. She was The Golden Icicle, she reminded herself as she rang for

Annette, and she'd frozen out men far more determined than the marquess.

Half an hour later she walked into the breakfast room to discover the others had already eaten and set out to explore the city. Feeling somewhat abandoned, she sat down, annoyed with both her family and herself. What on earth ailed her? she brooded, poking disconsolately at her food. She was accustomed to being alone, thrived on it, as a matter of fact, and these past few months had been rather a strain for her. Much as she loved her cousins, having someone constantly underfoot had been hard, and by rights she ought to be rejoicing at the unexpected freedom.

But she wasn't rejoicing. She was feeling lost, rejected, and yes, she admitted with a troubled sigh, lonely. These were all-too-familiar emotions, and ones she'd spent her adult life trying to escape. She'd considered that she was the better for it, but now she realized she'd only been deluding herself. The realization was enough to destroy the little appetite she had.

She spent the rest of the morning going over her books and answering her correspondence. When Lord Berwick arrived for their drive, she considered sending him on his way with a blunt message not to bother her again, but after a moment's thought, she changed her mind and decided to go with him. Anyone's company was preferable to her own, even if it was someone like Berwick.

He was waiting in the drawing room, and at the sight of her, he leapt to his feet. "I am pleased to see you have recovered from your illness," he told her, availing himself of her hand and carrying it to his lips. "I could hardly sleep a wink last night, I was so concerned."

"I am quite recovered, my lord," Belle replied drolly, thinking he looked rather bright-eyed and

pink-cheeked to have spent a sleepless night.
"Thank you for your concern."

"Not at all." For a moment she feared he was
going to pat her hand again, but he pressed another kiss to it instead. "Are you ready for our
drive? I've been looking forward to it all day."

"I'm sure you have." She was just able to keep
the sarcasm out of her voice. "But I'm afraid we
must wait for Annette to join us. She should only
be a moment."

"Annette?" The marquess's brows gathered in a
frown.

"My abigail." As his frown deepened into a
scowl, she added, "Surely, my lord, you didn't expect me to accompany you without a chaperon?"

The dark look he sent her made it obvious that
he did. "You are scarce a green girl, Miss Portham,
who must need guard her reputation with such fa-
natic devotion," he grumbled, some of his surface
charm dissipating. "It would hardly create a scandal for you to accompany me for a ride in an open
carriage."

"Perhaps not." The smile she gave him could
have frozen fire. "But that is a risk I choose not to
run. If you don't wish to wait, I quite understand.
Another time, perhaps?"

Berwick's hazel eyes narrowed, and Belle could
almost feel him weighing his options. His lips
firmed and he took a decisive step toward her. "A
ride is unnecessary, Miss Portham. I can say what
I have to say here as well as in my carriage; better,
for I shan't have to contend with some foolish servant listening to my every word."

Belle's sardonic amusement faded at the determined look on his face, and she began retreating
toward the door. "My lord, I do not think this is
wise—"

"I thought about pretending to have fallen in

love with you," he said coolly, continuing his advance, "but it is obvious you have as little use for that emotion as I do. Let us be blunt with each other, my dear. You have something I want, money, and I have something you want, my position in the House of Lords. It is only logical that we marry. Do you not agree?"

"I do not!" Belle gasped, horrified by the calculating proposal, and more horrified still to realize that once, she might have actually considered his offer.

"Why?" He looked faintly amused. "I have made a study of you, Miss Portham, and I know you better than you know yourself. With your little charities, and your dabbling in politics, you have been longing for the one thing even your great fortune cannot buy, and that is access to political power. Power which would be yours as my wife. Society marriages have been made with far less in common, so I see no reason why you should object. That is the reason you have been allowing Colford to dance attendance upon you, isn't it?" he added when she continued to stare at him.

"Marcus?" His name slipped unbidden from her lips. "He has not been dancing attendance upon me!"

"Come, my dear, do not play me for a fool. It is obvious he has been doing just that, and more obvious still that you have been encouraging his suit. The world knows he was courting Lady Bingington for her pocketbook, and when she didn't come up to scratch, he turned his sights on you. If you'll consider him, then why not me?"

Belle's heart gave an odd lurch, not from fear but from shock. In that moment she knew she loved Marcus, and the realization filled her with joy and overwhelming terror. She was still struggling with the startling revelation when Lord Berwick stopped in front of her to take her hand in his.

"I realize this is rather unexpected," he said, his expression cool as he studied her face, "but I am afraid I can no longer afford to be patient. I have certain pressing debts in need of settling, and the sooner our betrothal is announced, the better I shall like it. Well, what say you, Miss Portham? Will you marry me?"

Belle's tangled emotions gave way to indignation as she glared at the marquess. "I think not, my lord," she returned coolly, furious that he should think she would consider so insulting a proposal. She knew she had a reputation for being a cold fish, but it hadn't occurred to her that she might also have the reputation of a fool. A woman would have to be a spiritless gudgeon to accept so calculating an offer! she thought with mounting anger.

"Are you certain?" Berwick raised a mocking eyebrow in response to her refusal. "I am offering you everything you have ever wanted in a marriage. You would be foolish beyond permission to refuse me merely because I haven't wrapped everything in fine linen to please your womanly pride."

His audacity left Belle temporarily speechless. "How do you know what I want?" she demanded once she'd regained the use of her tongue. "You don't even know me!"

"Because, my sweet, as I have already said, I have been studying you. How else do you think I knew you would be in St. John's Wood that day?"

Belle stared at him, and in a flash the realization hit her. "You cut the reins to my carriage!" she accused, shocked that he should so casually admit his guilt.

"I wished to meet you, and place you in my debt if at all possible," he replied, unrepentant. "A rather trite scheme, I grant you, but an effective one."

Fury such as she had never known filled Belle. Since her great-aunt's death, her fortune had stood between her and the rest of the world. She thought she'd learned to accept the pain this isolation sometimes caused, but until this very moment, she never realized the anger that paralleled the pain. Anger that burned as brightly as an inferno, and was now threatening to engulf her.

It was tempting, so sweetly tempting to double up her fist and . . . What was the saying? She searched her mind before coming up with the cant expression . . . "plant him a facer." Yes, that was it. She would plant him a facer and then watch in smug pleasure as he howled with pain. For a moment she almost gave in to the impulse, but at the last minute she managed to contain herself. If he thought her so coldly calculating that she would buy a husband as she would a gown or a carriage, she saw no reason why she should disillusion him. She took a step back from him, her lips curling in a smile of polite regret.

"Your scheme may have been trite, Lord Berwick," she said dulcetly, "but I would hardly term it effective. I had no idea that you would entertain an offer for me, and now I am afraid it is too late."

"Too late?"

"Yes." She gave a weary sigh. "I have already selected a husband, you see, and as I've a great deal of capital sunk into the expenditure, I really cannot cry off now. As a man of superior reasoning, you surely will understand."

"What do you mean you have already selected a husband?" Berwick demanded in outrage. It was obvious he'd come expecting his offer of marriage to be accepted, and that this development was not at all to his liking. "Who have you selected?"

"Why, Lord Colford, of course," she drawled, delighted to see the wretch squirming in impotent fury. "You say the world knows he has set his sights on me, but perhaps it didn't occur to the world that it was I who set my sights on him. And really, I am getting both him and his foolish cousin for such a bargain price, I couldn't possibly resist."

Berwick's face turned purple, and for an uneasy moment Belle feared he would strike her. He even took a tentative step toward her before coming to an abrupt halt, his eyes straying past her shoulder to the doorway. An ugly sneer twisted his lips as he glanced back to Belle.

"My apologies, Miss Portham, for misreading the situation," he said, his voice sharp with contempt. "Now, if you will pardon me, I shall leave you alone to enjoy your latest acquisition. I wish you both the joy of each other."

A frisson of unease stole down Belle's spine at his cruel jibe. She turned slowly around, and her worst fears were confirmed at the sight of a white-faced Marcus standing in the doorway.

Twelve

A terrible silence filled the room as Lord Berwick brushed past Marcus and Belle, visibly pleased with the havoc he had caused. Simon and St. Ives stood behind Marcus, but after exchanging grim looks, they quietly withdrew, leaving them alone. Belle was the first to recover, her heart pounding as she nervously wet her lips.

"Marcus ... I ..." Her voice trailed off, and she drew a shaky breath. "This isn't what you think ..."

"Isn't it?" His voice was thick with bitterness as he studied her. He'd never felt such pain, such a deep, burning sense of betrayal, and the agony of it was almost more than he could endure.

"No." She shook her head, apprehension making her stomach clench as she fought down the nausea that threatened to overwhelm her. There had to be some way she could explain, some way she could make him understand, she thought, frantically searching for the proper words. But fear held her tongue and mind prisoner, and she could only stare at him in helpless confusion, unable to find a way to undo the terrible damage she had done.

Marcus sensed her struggle and gave her a hard, cruel smile. "Strange you should be at such a loss

192

for words now, Miss Portham. You certainly weren't suffering a lack of them when you were describing to Berwick how you had purchased me."

Belle's numbing horror gave way to a flash of desperate anger. "I was only trying to be rid of him!" she cried, taking a stumbling step forward. "He had just proposed to me in the most calculating way."

"And you refused him?" Marcus said, his own pain making him lash out. "I should have thought such an offer to be just to your liking. What happened? Did the good marquess prove to be too expensive for even your deep pockets?"

The caustic observation brought Belle's head snapping up with fury. "How dare you!" she cried, her hands clenching in fists. "You have no right to say such things to me!"

"No right?" Marcus gave a harsh laugh, his love twisting like a knife in his chest. When he thought of how he worshiped her, adored her, thought her so far above his touch, and all the time she was scheming to purchase him as casually as her cousin had bought Gray Boy last week. He sent her a furious look as realization dawned.

"It was you," he said coldly, almost hating her in that moment. "You bought up my debts, didn't you?"

Evasion was beyond Belle. "Yes," she admitted, not trying to hide the tears that were filling her eyes. "But not for the reasons you think. Not to buy you. I—I only wanted to help . . ."

That hurt even more, to know she regarded him as nothing more than one of her charities. "Help yourself to my title, you mean," he snapped, his lips curling in a brutal sneer. "You are the same as any Cit, Miss Portham, thinking your gold can

buy you anything you desire. Well, you are wrong.
It cannot buy *me!*"

Belle could only gaze at him, her heart shatter-
ing at the fury blazing in his silver eyes. Part of
her was coolly amused he should accuse her of using her fortune to buy him when, in truth, her fortune had driven him away . . . just as it had driven
everyone away. The other part of her wanted to
slap his arrogant face, and then beg him to love
her. The opposing emotions almost overwhelmed
her, and she panicked, retreating behind her safe
wall of impenetrable ice.

"Can I not?" she asked, her voice filled with
mocking superiority. "In that case, I suppose I
ought to cut my losses and move on to some other
game. You owe me twenty thousand pounds, my
lord. I shall expect payment within a month." And
with that she brushed past him, her blond head
held high.

"You're mad. It is the only possible explanation
that makes any sense," Pip said, her lips pursed as
she paced up and down Belle's sitting room. "Only
last year you were trying to buy a viscount, and
now you're out bargaining for an earl. Really, Belle,
have your wits gone begging?"

"I wasn't bargaining for Marcus," Belle denied
tearfully, her head turned from Pip as she gazed
out the window. Less than twenty minutes had
passed since the scene in the parlor, but she felt as
if she'd aged a hundred years. She'd thought the
loss of her parents the most wrenching pain she
would ever feel, but even those staggering losses
were nothing compared to what she was feeling
now.

"Well, you certainly couldn't prove it by me!"
Pip grumbled, scowling at her friend. She and the
others had been waiting in the front sitting room

when they'd heard Marcus storm out, and while
Alex had given chase, Pip had come upstairs expecting to find Belle in a similar rage. Instead
she'd found her curled up on her chaise lounge,
sobbing as if her heart would break.

It had taken less than a few minutes to wheedle
the story from her, and her worried concern
turned to impatience at Belle's stammering confession. After a year of marriage, Pip was no stranger
to male pride, and she could only imagine what
the earl suffered when he learned the woman he
loved had bought up his vowels. And Colford did
love Belle; Pip knew that as surely as she knew
Belle loved him. Lord, what a hopeless tangle, she
thought, plopping down onto a chair beside the
chaise.

"Belle," she began, her voice gentle, "why did
you pay off his lordship's loans if not to put him
in your debt? Was it because of Toby and Julia?"

Belle shook her head, dabbing at her eyes with
her sodden handkerchief. "I wanted to help," she
repeated wearily, hating herself now for the foolish impulse. "He had worked so hard, Pip, so very
hard. It didn't seem fair he should lose everything
because of his wastrel of a father. I thought if I
bought up his notes, it would give him the opportunity to make something of Colford. I never
meant he should be indebted to me, only ... only
that he should be free."

Pip believed her at once, for despite her coolness, Belle was one of the kindest and most giving
people she had ever met. Still, she knew there had
to be more to the story, and she leaned forward to
take Belle's hands in hers. "And because you love
him," she said gently, her green eyes soft with
understanding. "Don't you, Belle?"

Belle's eyes filled as a fresh wave of unhappiness washed over her. "Yes, I love him," she con-

fessed, her heart convulsing with pain. "And I have lost him, Pip. I have lost him."

"You wished to see me, my lord?" Toby asked, his brown eyes wary as he took in the sight of Marcus sprawled in his club chair. He'd just returned from dropping Julia and Mrs. Larksdale at their house when the butler had informed him that his cousin was in his study and wished to speak with him. The tone of the butler's voice had indicated something momentous was afoot, and he wondered uneasily if it had anything to do with him.

"Ah yes, Toby, old friend." Marcus hailed him expansively, waving his snifter of brandy in greeting. "Come join me in a toast."

"Toast to what?" Toby demanded with a suspicious scowl. His cousin had discarded his jacket, and his cravat lay in ruins about his tanned throat. As he drew nearer, Toby could see the dark flush staining Colford's cheeks, and there was a dangerous glitter in his eyes that made Toby uneasy. He sniffed cautiously, and his eyebrows rose. "Good God, Colford, you're foxed!"

Marcus took another mouthful of brandy. "Don't be an ass, Toby," he grumbled into his glass. "I've scarce had a drop."

"Rot, you're jug-bitten as a duke!" Toby accused, shocked to see his usually fastidious cousin so disguised. He tried to think what could have brought him to such a state, and then swallowed uneasily as various explanations occurred to him.

"Nothing wrong, is there?" he asked, settling his bulk on the chair facing Marcus's desk. "Estate ain't going to be overrun by bailiffs or anything of the sort?"

"Not yet," Marcus replied with another harsh laugh, "but it is only a matter of weeks. I have been informed by Miss Portham that I have until the end of the month to repay my debts or she will move against the estate."

"Miss Portham? What has she to do with things?" Toby asked, more certain than ever that Marcus was bosky.

"Everything. She is the 'mysterious benefactor' who bought up my vowels."

The bitter clarity of the words wiped the frown from Toby's face. He knew his cousin had been brooding over the identity of whoever had settled his debts, but he'd dismissed the grumbling complaints as looking a gift horse in the mouth. Now he wished he'd paid more attention. "Why would she do that?" he asked, nervously wiping his hands on his nankeens.

"How the devil do I know?" Marcus demanded with a snarl, his fingers clenching around his glass. After he had stormed out of Belle's house, Alex had tried stopping him; tried explaining that Belle's motives were purely unselfish, but he'd angrily shaken him off. He'd felt the burning in his eyes, and the knowledge she could wield such power over his emotions had only added to the fury devouring him. How could she have done this to him? he wondered savagely. How could she have betrayed him?

"Do you think she'll forbid Julia to see me?" Toby asked, eyeing the brandy decanter wistfully. He longed for a sip, but something told him that it might be best if one of them at least kept his senses clear.

"I shouldn't be surprised," Marcus retorted, knowing the words were untrue even as he was muttering them. "Not that it would matter. Dolitan is her guardian, and so long as you have his approval, there's not a blessed thing she can do. Unless . . ." His voice trailed off as a sudden thought occurred to him.

"Unless?" Toby pressed, leaning closer.

Marcus thrust his hand through his thick hair, adding to his dissipated appearance. "Dolitan knows about the kidnapping," he confessed, and then at Toby's horrified look, he added, "He doesn't know about your part in it, but if that should change, I wouldn't give your engagement to Julia a condemned man's chance for salvation."

"But that was an accident!" Toby all but wailed, his knee connecting painfully with the table as he leapt to his feet. "I ain't the one who knocked her on the head!"

"I hardly think that will hold much weight with Dolitan," Marcus replied sardonically, remembering the hard look that had stolen across Simon's face when he'd spoken softly of vengeance. "But I wouldn't worry; unless Miss Portham wants a forced marriage, I much doubt she'll say anything."

"Eh?" Toby asked, bending over to rub his aching knee. "What do you mean?"

Marcus set his glass down. Now that he'd had some time to recover his temper, he knew Belle hadn't been trying to purchase him. Doubtless it was just as she said, that she was only trying to help, but the pain of it still tore at him. No man who counted himself such wanted the woman he loved to save him from ruin, he admitted glumly, wishing he hadn't had so much to drink. Damn, but it was hard to think . . .

"Marcus." Toby was gazing at him beseechingly. "What do you mean Miss Portham will hold her tongue unless she wants to be forced into marriage? Never say I would have to *marry* her!" he demanded, his voice quavering at the very thought.

"Of course not, you simpleton," Marcus retorted with an angry glare. "I am talking about myself. Miss Portham regained consciousness in my house, and if word of it got out, there would be no hope but marriage for either of us."

"Oh." Toby sat back down, his expression thoughtful. Odd place, Society, he mused in his ponderous way. A married man could have a dozen mistresses or a married lady a dozen lovers, and the *ton* scarce batted an eye. But let an unmarried man and an unmarried lady pass more than five minutes alone together, and they were ruined. It made no earthly sense.

He thought of last year's contretemps when Kingsford had sought to compromise Viscount St. Ives and Miss Lambert by arranging for them to spend the night in the same room. Disaster had been mysteriously prevented, but it had been a near thing. Had Miss Portham been discovered unconscious at his cousin's home, the results would have been much the same, so it was probably just as well things had turned out as they had. Or was it . . . His brows met in a scowl as the germ of an idea sprouted in the fertile soil of his poetic mind. What if . . .

"Belle, dearest, how are you feeling?" Georgiana's voice was filled with concern as she poked her head into Belle's sitting room. "Is your poor head still giving you fits?"

Belle pried open one eye, studying the intruder with grim resignation. She wondering bleakly how her cousin would react if she tossed her bodily from her room, and then decided she wasn't up to such a futile endeavor. Georgiana, being Georgiana, would only walk right back in.

"Just a little," she prevaricated, deciding it wasn't really a lie. Her head was pounding as it always did when she was upset, but it wasn't anything she couldn't endure. It was the cold, empty ache in the center of her chest that worried her most, for the pain of it would surely kill her.

"Hmp, well, whatever is ailing you, I fear it must be contagious," Georgiana grumbled, walking into the room and sitting on one of the chairs with a sigh. "Julia has closeted herself in her room, and I've not so much as caught a glimpse of her all day."

"Julia is ill?" Belle asked, struggling up from the black morass of her own misery to feel a glimmer of concern.

"Sulking, more like it," Georgiana said with a sniff. "Since you and Colford had your mysterious falling out, she and Toby have been squabbling like a couple of children. He sent her a note this morning, and she went dashing up to her rooms in tears."

"What?" Belle cried, leaping to her feet and glaring at her cousin. "When was this? Why wasn't I told?"

"The note was delivered after breakfast," Georgiana replied with an indifferent shrug. "And you wasn't told because you'd sent word down you was ill. I wasn't about to trouble you over something so trifling as a lovers' quarrel."

"I'd hardly call it 'trifling' if it had Julia in tears," Belle replied sharply, wincing as a pang of guilt stabbed at her. She knew her estrangement from Marcus had hurt more than the two of them, and the knowledge added to her pain.

"Nonsense," Georgiana corrected in her blunt manner, "all couples have their little differences. Just leave them alone, and I guarantee they'll soon be billing and cooing like a pair of turtledoves."

"But what if they aren't?" Belle demanded, pacing the room in mounting agitation. She accepted the painful fact that she'd already destroyed any chance of happiness she might have known with Marcus, and she couldn't bear to think she might have done the same to Julia and Toby.

"Then they aren't." Georgiana's negligent shrug indicated her apathy. "Really, Belle, I fail to see why you are getting so upset over this. In the event they do decide to break their engagement, there's nothing we can do about it."

Belle stopped abruptly, some of the fire returning to her eyes. Her fear and blindness had caused enough unhappiness, she decided with determination. She was hanged if she would allow it to cause any more. "Isn't there?" she said, her chin coming up with conviction. "We shall just see about that!" And she turned and stormed out of the room, so furious that she didn't notice the cunning smile curving Georgiana's lips.

"No. Absolutely not."

"Blast it, Colford, must you be such a stubborn ass?" Simon's eyes glittered with frustration as he glared at the earl. "This isn't charity I am offering, but a simple business proposition. If you'd put aside that bloody pride of yours for two minutes, you would see that!"

Marcus returned Simon's angry look, his jaw clenching as he fought to control his temper. He and Dolitan had been locked in his study for the better part of the afternoon, struggling to work out a financial arrangement, and his temper was beginning to fray, along with his patience.

"You may call it whatever you like, Dolitan," he said, his voice cold with painful control, "but I refuse to allow a woman to settle my debts. I'd rather die a pauper than allow that."

"I've explained that Belle would not be the one to settle your precious debts," Simon said, leaning forward to rest his hands on the polished surface of Marcus's desk. "I will buy them from her, and then turn them over to you in return for your agreement to act as my partner. There is no charity here, my lord, no special favors. I shall expect you to work damned hard for your money, the same as I would of any man."

Marcus pinched the bridge of his nose, his silver eyes closing as weariness washed over him. In the two days since the bitter confrontation in Belle's drawing room, he doubted he'd slept more than a few hours, and the lack of sleep was catching up with him. He felt tired, harassed from all sides, and almost desperate with unhappiness. The proposition Dolitan was offering him was sweetly tempting, and the logical part of his mind knew he would be a fool to say no. Unfortunately the illogical, emotional part of his mind held temporary sway, and he wanted only to be left alone.

"Dolitan," he began wearily, "I thank you for your help, but—"

The door to his study flew open and Belle dashed inside, the white cast to her skin bringing both men to their feet.

"Belle, what is it?" Marcus reached her first, his hands closing around her chilled fingers. "What has happened?"

Belle turned to him, seeking the reassuring comfort of his touch. "It is Julia," she said, her voice trembling as she held out a letter to him. "Oh, Marcus, she and Toby have eloped!"

"*What?*" He took the letter from her and tore it open, his lips thinning as he read the hastily penned lined.

"*Dearest, dearest Belle,*" he read aloud,

"*By the time you receive this, Toby and I shall be on our way to Gretna Green. We know it is wrong, but we could not bear the chance that we should be parted. We*

*love both you and Lord Colford, and hope that one day
you shall find it in your heart to forgive us.*

   Love Always,

   Julia"

"It is all my fault," Belle mourned, her eyes
misting as she studied his strained features. He
looked as miserable and unhappy as she felt, and
the knowledge added to the burden of guilt
weighing her down. Blinking back tears, she laid a
trembling hand on his arm. "I am sorry, Marcus,"
she said softly. "So very sorry."

Her contrite words and the touch of her hand
brought his head snapping up. "Sorry?" he repeated incredulously, meeting her tear-drenched
gaze. "My God, Belle, you've done nothing to
apologize for! This is Toby's and Julia's folly, not
yours!"

She wanted to believe him, but in her heart she
knew the blame was hers. "But if I hadn't quar-
reled with you, if I hadn't hurt you, they would
never have run away," she said, her hand dropping to her side as she glanced uneasily away.
"You read what she wrote; she suspects us of attempting to part them. She'd never have felt that
if . . . if it hadn't been for me."

"Nonsense," Marcus began firmly, determined
to shoulder his own share of guilt. "I ought to
have known something was up this morning
when Toby talked to me. I—"

"This mutual self-abasement is all very interesting," Simon interrupted with a dark scowl, "but
it's not doing a bloody thing to get my sister
back." He turned to Marcus. "When Flanders
talked to you this morning, did he say anything,
anything at all, which in hindsight might have indicated he was planning an elopement?"

Marcus frowned, trying to remember what Toby
had said. "I'm not sure," he admitted, thrusting a

hand through his hair. "He was prattling on about poetry, as he usually does, and talking about going up to Grasmere to visit Dove Cottage, but I—" He broke off abruptly.

"What is it? Have you remembered something?" Simon demanded, crowding closer.

"He made mention of one of our distant cousins, the widow of a country vicar who lives outside of Coventry," he said slowly, recalling the nervous look on his cousin's face as he spoke of the elderly woman. "He asked if I'd heard from her recently, and if she still had the tenancy on the house. I told him that she had, and he let the matter drop. At the time I thought he was hinting he wished to use it for his bridal trip, but now ..."

"Coventry is on the road north," Simon interposed, his expression grim. "Perhaps they mean to break their journey there. Would this woman shelter them?"

"Probably," Marcus admitted, already making plans to travel north and intercept the fleeing couple. "She was always fond of Toby, although I can't imagine her countenancing a runaway match. But at least she would be there to lend an air of respectability to the thing."

"Give me her direction," Simon ordered decisively, already starting toward the door. "I've several horses and carriages posted at various inns on the Great Road, and I should be able to overtake them within a few hours. Belle, it would probably be best if you came with me. Julia is bound to be in a state, and I'll need you there to comfort her."

"One moment," Marcus protested, his expression every bit as grim as Simon's. "What about me? If you think I intend letting you hare after my cousin with murder on your mind, you're much mistaken. I'm going with you."

Simon sent him an impatient look. "I'd hoped

you might take one of the other roads in the event they chose a different route, my lord," he said, not bothering to deny his lethal intentions. "It makes no sense for all three of us to make the same journey in the same carriage when we could well be wasting our time."

"Then you and Miss Portham take the alternative route," Marcus insisted stubbornly, although he found the notion of Belle and the handsome Simon sharing the intimate confines of a carriage displeasing. "Besides, Mrs. Atherton is most distrusting of strangers, and I doubt she would grant you entrance."

"Perhaps I could go alone," Belle suggested, vaguely annoyed they should discuss her as if she weren't there. "The two of you could check the other roads for any sign of them, and—"

"No!" Both men spoke decisively and at once. They glared at each other for a long moment before Simon gave a weary sigh.

"You and Belle take the Great Road," he said to Marcus, "and I will do some discreet checking here. I've been thinking, and unless they're foolish enough to take the mail coach, they'll have need to hire a private carriage. I'll look into that while the two of you pursue the truants."

It took several more minutes of haggling, but Marcus and Belle were soon on their way north in Simon's opulent carriage. Belle sat across from him, her posture stiff and wary, and he wondered uneasily if she was worried about the impropriety of the situation. He cleared his throat and gave her an anxious look.

"Miss Portham, if you are worried about our traveling without benefit of a chaperon, I assure you I have no intention of revealing a word of this to anyone. Your reputation is quite safe with me."

Belle stirred uneasily, her eyes lowering to her

tightly clenched hands as she fought back a fresh
flow of tears. When she thought of the cruel asper-
sions she'd cast against him, she felt sunk with
shame. Even if she hadn't loved him with all her
heart, she would have felt the same guilty re-
morse, for if there was anything she did know, it
was that Colford was a man of impeccable honor.
She had questioned that honor, and now there was
nothing left to do but to apologize.

"Lord Colford ... Marcus," she began, raising
solemn golden-brown eyes to meet his, "there is
something I should like to say to you. Something
I should have said days ago ..."

Marcus watched her closely, seeing the contri-
tion and the determination on her lovely features.
He knew she was about to beg his forgiveness for
her actions, and he knew he couldn't bear it. He'd
rather have her contempt than her pity, he decided, reaching out to lay a gloved finger against
her lips.

"No, Belle," he said, his voice low as he gently
brushed his finger back and forth over her trembling lips. "No words. We only seem to tangle ourselves up in them, so perhaps it would be best if
we said nothing at all."

His tone and the sweet touch of his hand shattered Belle's control. "But, Marcus, I—"

"Please." He gave her a sad smile, his heart
pounding with helpless love as he committed her
beautiful face to memory. "I know you have no regard for me, but I beg you, not another word."

Belle gazed at him, her anguish giving way to
hot anger. She'd endured so much this past week,
and now he dared sit there and calmly tell her that
she had no regard for him. The thought of it filled
her with a deep, burning rage, and she slapped his
hand away, twenty years of controlling her emotions erupting in an explosive flash.

"No regard for you?" she repeated incredulously, her eyes narrowing in fury. "How can you say such a thing, you ... you dolt! I love you!"

At first Marcus could only stare at her, certain he had finally gone mad. Certainly she didn't look like a lady who had just declared her love, he thought dazedly, studying her features with awe. Her cheeks were flushed with fury, and her full mouth was set in a mulish pout that made him want to shout with laughter. The golden eyes he'd seen filled with cool contempt now sparkled like topaz, and she looked as if she'd like nothing better than to claw out his eyes. He took a deep breath, praying he wasn't about to make a complete ass out of himself.

"You love me?"

"Of course I love you!" Belle snapped, her temper flaring free of all constraint. It felt glorious to finally speak her mind, and she did so with relish, not giving a single thought to the possible consequences.

"Why else do you think I bought up those wretched debts of yours?" she demanded, poking her finger against his chest. "I may be wealthier than you, but I'm hardly so well heeled that I go about squandering twenty thousand pounds on people I don't like! I wanted to help you, curse you, and that was the only thing I could think of to do!"

"You love me." He repeated the words, disbelief turning to wonder. It was all his dreams come true, and for a moment he was too afraid to believe in the miracle of it. If he was wrong, the pain of it would kill him.

"Must you sit there repeating everything?" Belle demanded impatiently, crowding closer until they were nose to nose. "I've just told you I love you, blast it, and I demand to know what you intend doing about it! Well?" she added in bellicose terms when he remained silent. "Do you love me or not?"

Marcus stared at her, his fears and doubts dissolving under a wave of sweet relief. He gave an exultant cry, his arms closing about her as he pulled her onto his lap. She gave a startled gasp, but even as his mouth was descending toward hers, her arms were closing around his neck in a fervent embrace.

Her lips were soft and sweet beneath his own, and he took them with equal parts desperation and desire. Everything he was or ever would be was in that kiss, and he would accept nothing less in return. He deepened the contact, his tongue teasing hers until he felt her shy response.

"Belle, Belle, my sweet, I love you," he whispered, his voice ragged with emotion. "I don't give a damn if you are as rich as a nabob or as poor as a pauper, I love you."

The fervent words brought tears of joy to Belle's eyes, but she wasn't yet ready to discard her anger. "You know you must marry me now," she told him with a fierce scowl. "You have compromised me, and if you refuse to do the honorable thing, I shall tell Simon, and—" She was silenced by another kiss.

Marcus was smiling provocatively when he raised his head again. "There is no reason to threaten me with your ferocious cousin, my love," he said, his thumb tracing lazy circles against the pulse pounding in her slender neck. "I would marry you if it meant going against a hundred Simons. But you are wrong to say I have compromised you; 'tis quite the other way around. You did tell Berwick you paid good money for me, you know, and now my reputation is quite ruined. I am a fallen man."

His joking reference to the debts made her blush guiltily. "I am sorry, Marcus," she said, her eyes dropping to her hands now resting on his broad chest. "I never meant to insult you; truly I did not. But the debts had you backed into a corner, and I couldn't bear to see you lose everything you had fought so hard to keep. I was only trying to—"

"—help," he finished, pressing a soft kiss to the top of her head. "I know, and I thank you for your kindness."

"You do?" She tilted back her head to gaze up at him.

"I do," he assured her, unable to resist the temptation of her parted lips. After another kiss, he drew back to give her a loving smile. "Not that I intend letting you pay my debts, mind. Simon had just made me a rather interesting offer before you came barging into my study, and I believe I shall take him up on it. How do you feel about being married to a country gentleman who raises horses, my love?"

Belle smiled mistily, happier than she had ever been in her life. For years she had held life and love at arm's length, refusing to believe she would ever know their sweetness. Now all she wanted was sitting beside her, and all she had to do was reach out and take it. For a moment all her old fears and insecurities threatened to overwhelm her, but one look at Marcus's face and they dissolved like morning mist. She reached up and gently tugged his head down to her.

"So long as that country gentleman is you, I can think of nothing I would like more," she said, and feeling greatly daring, pressed a kiss to his mouth.

They continued their journey north, alternately kissing and making lazy plans for the future. Belle's cloak and bonnet lay on the opposite bench, joined by Marcus's greatcoat and gloves as they snuggled in congenial contentment. But despite her own happiness, Belle could not help but worry about Julia and Toby. She mentioned her fears to Marcus and was surprised when he gave a soft chuckle.

"I shouldn't worry so much about them, my love," he said, running a hand through her delightfully mussed curls. "Toby is such a notorious cloth-head, I much doubt he managed to get them out of London, let alone all the way to Coventry. We'll tarry long enough to question Mrs. Atherton, and then we'd best be making our way back to London before we are forced to spend the night on the road. Our marriage will cause talk enough, but I'll not have a scrap of scandal attached to your good name."

His determination to protect her warmed Belle's heart, and she was about to say as much when a sudden thought intruded. She tried brushing it aside, but it would not move, and the more she thought of it, the more suspicious she became. She lifted her head from Marcus's shoulder and gave him a thoughtful frown. "Marcus, may I ask you something?"

"Certainly, my love; what is it?" he asked, his heart filled with peaceful satisfaction.

"Doesn't it strike you as odd that Simon would allow me to accompany you without so much as a maid to lend us countenance?"

Marcus's contentment vanished at the question. "There wasn't time," he said, his brows gathering in a frown as he considered the matter. "It is a trifle unconventional, I suppose, but ..." His voice tapered off and his frown deepened. "No, you're right. It is damned odd he would allow such a thing."

"Especially if you knew Simon's past," Belle said, hoping her cousin would forgive her for violating his confidence. "There were rumors about his mother shortly after his birth, and he has always been more sensitive than most about such things. I find it difficult to believe he would blithely let us take off across the country without so much as a word of protest. He must have known it would cause talk."

"And he seemed rather sanguine about his sister's elopement," Marcus added thoughtfully, remembering the other man's response. "Not at all the sort of reaction one would expect from a man of Dolitan's stamp. Yet why would he have wanted to throw us together like this? It doesn't make sense."

The answer to their question came some twenty minutes later when they reached the small cottage tucked into the woods just outside of Coventry. They found Julia and Toby, all right, but the younger couple was far from alone. In addition to a smiling Georgiana, the errant lovers were joined by Lord and Lady St. Ives, and a rather smug-faced Simon, who was regarding them with obvious satisfaction.

"It is about time you arrived," he accused them with a lazy smile. "You were so long, we were beginning to think you had lost your way."

"We may have taken a wrong turn here and there, but as you can see, we have finally arrived at the desired location," Marcus observed cryptically, slipping an arm about Belle's shoulder. "This is a group conspiracy, I take it?"

"It was my idea, actually," Toby confessed, preening with pride at his cleverness. "Figured it was the easiest way to get the pair of you safely shackled. Worked before." He slid a nervous look in the viscount's direction.

Alex ignored him with lordly indifference. "We decided a frontal assault wasn't the safest way of achieving our objective," he said with the ease of a man accustomed to thinking in military terms. "Subterfuge was clearly indicated, and while Dolitan mounted his rearguard action, we lay our ambush."

"Brilliant as always, St. Ives," Marcus commended him with a laugh. "I can see why your superiors thought so highly of you. It is a brilliant plan, but I am afraid it is all for naught."

"What do you mean for naught?" Julia demanded, sounding surprisingly like her elder brother. "You have just passed several hours in a closed carriage with my cousin, sir, and from the blush on her cheeks, I'd wager that time wasn't spent in idle conversation! You have compromised her, and if you do not do the honorable thing, Toby shall call you out! Won't you, Toby?" She glanced to her chosen knight for verification.

"Eh?" He gave a nervous start and studied his older cousin's powerful physique with decided trepidation. "Er ... quite so, m'love, be glad to. No offense, Colford," he added hastily, least the other man take umbrage.

"None taken." Marcus inclined his head graciously. "But your Herculean efforts on our behalf are wasted as Belle and I have already decided to marry. Haven't we?" And he ducked his head to kiss Belle in front of their gaping witnesses.

While Belle and Marcus exchanged a warm kiss, the others erupted into excited babble, talking eagerly amongst themselves as they made plans to announced the coming nuptials. The couple in question ignored them, lost in a sensual world of their own making. Pledges already spoken were now silently made, and when Marcus finally raised his head, his eyes shone with love.

"We shall announce our engagement tomorrow night at Julia's ball," he said, his eyes not leaving

Belle's. "And we shall marry by week's end, provided I can secure a special license."

"That shouldn't be too difficult," Alex said, producing a document from his pocket. "I have a friend in Doctor's Commons," he explained when Simon gave him a startled look. "It never hurts to be prepared."

"Then the end of the week it shall be," Marcus replied with a laugh, turning his attention back to Belle. "Unless you have some objection, my love?" he added somewhat anxiously.

The emotion in his voice melted the last of the ice that had imprisoned her for so long. Feeling freer and happier than she had in her whole life, she gently cupped Marcus's face in her hands. "The only objection I have is that the end of the week seems a lifetime away," she said softly, her lips curving in a smile of glowing love. "But I suppose I can wait . . . if I must."

And then, with the people closest to her in all the world looking on, she kissed the man she loved, embracing life and all its pains and pleasures with unrestrained joy. The Golden Icicle had melted at last.

Avon Regency Romance

Kasey Michaels

THE CHAOTIC MISS CRISPINO
76300-1/$3.99 US/$4.99 Can

THE DUBIOUS MISS DALRYMPLE
89908-6/$2.95 US/$3.50 Can

THE HAUNTED MISS HAMPSHIRE
76301-X/$3.99 US/$4.99 Can

THE WAGERED MISS WINSLOW
76302-8/$3.99 US/$4.99 Can

Loretta Chase

THE ENGLISH WITCH 70660-1/$2.95 US/$3.50 Can
ISABELLA 70597-4/$2.95 US/$3.95 Can
KNAVES' WAGER 71363-2/$3.95 US/$4.95 Can
THE SANDALWOOD PRINCESS
71455-8/$3.99 US/$4.99 Can
THE VISCOUNT VAGABOND
70836-1/$2.95 US/$3.50 Can

Jo Beverley

EMILY AND THE DARK ANGEL
71555-4/$3.99 US/$4.99 Can

THE STANFORTH SECRETS
71438-8/$3.99 US/$4.99 Can